BANKER'S ALIBI
A Cybil Quindt Mystery
Ilsa Mayr

Apprentice investigator Cybil Quindt, on the trail of an embezzler, goes undercover as a teller in a small town bank. Unlike her previous case, which escalated from petty theft to murder, Cybil is certain her newest case will be a safe and simple assignment—much to the delight of both her mother and her estranged husband.

However, days after Cybil begins at the bank, one of the other tellers is found dead. The authorities rule the death a suicide but when Cybil is assigned to deal with the dead woman's estate, the investigator uncovers secrets which contradict the official verdict. Cybil suspects foul play and once again throws herself into an investigation marked by blackmail, murder and mayhem.

BANKER'S ALIBI

•

Ilsa Mayr

AVALON BOOKS
NEW YORK

Published by Thomas Bouregy & Co., Inc.
160 Madison Avenue, New York, NY 10016

Library of Congress Cataloging-in-Publication Data

Mayr, Ilsa.
    Banker's alibi / Ilsa Mayr.
        p. cm. — (Cybil Quindt mystery series)
    ISBN-13: 978-0-8034-9819-8 (hardcover : alk. paper)
    ISBN-10: 0-8034-9819-5 (hardcover : alk. paper) 1. Women
private investigators—Fiction. 2. Banks and banking—Fiction.
3. Embezzlement—Fiction. 4. Indiana—Fiction. I. Title.

PS3613.A97B36 2007
813'.6—dc22

                                                                2006029679

PRINTED IN THE UNITED STATES OF AMERICA
ON ACID-FREE PAPER
BY HADDON CRAFTSMEN, BLOOMSBURG, PENNSYLVANIA

This book is dedicated to my children,
Dominique and Philip.

Chapter One

I had counted the stack of one-dollar bills four times and had come up with four different sums. I wanted to put my head down on the counter in the teller's cage and indulge in a good cry. "Cybil Quindt, don't you dare cry," I whispered to myself.

In the hundred-and-ten-year history of the Westport National Bank I'm sure no manager trainee had ever disgraced the bank by bursting into tears of frustration. Except I wasn't a real manager trainee. Just posing as one. If my ability to count bills was anything to go by, I'd never be an efficient teller.

Nine days ago the vice president of Westport's major bank and my old school friend, Joan Bower, came to the Keller Security Agency where I am an apprentice investigator and asked if she could hire us to look quietly into irregularities at Westport's branch bank in Victoria Grove, Indiana. Irregularities, she confessed with a pale face and a worried voice, that had to do with dormant accounts.

When Barney Keller, owner of the agency and my boss and uncle, asked why she didn't contact the police, her face grew even paler. I was afraid she'd pass out, but with a visible effort she pulled herself together. Apparently banks will go to great lengths to keep the news of embezzling by employees a secret from their clients. She muttered something about this being like the fox living in the henhouse.

As Joan explained it and as I understood it, if there was no activity in an account for seven years, the account escheated to the state. Escheat. A neat word I had to look up. It meant revert. In the sixth year of a dormant account, a letter was sent to the owner, informing him or her of the possible loss of funds. Then, if nothing was done by the end of the year, the state got the money. According to Joan, one of the tellers at the Victoria Grove branch had been helping herself, or himself, to money from these accounts just before they were marked dormant and could thus be flagged and watched.

Often these accounts belonged to elderly people who considered them as "safe" nest eggs, earmarked for emergencies. What a shock it had to be to discover that these accounts had been all but emptied.

Uncle Barney thought I'd be perfect for the undercover job at the branch bank. That's why I was here, counting crumpled bills for the fifth time.

Manager trainees have to spend time in all sections of the bank, which was perfect for the snooping I had to do. Not so perfect for customers who ended up at my window and had to endure my slow, laborious counting of bills and coins.

"Cybil, are you having trouble?" Heather Atkins asked.

Heather worked in the teller's cage to my right. "Not any more," I said. My fifth count tallied with my first and that was good enough for me.

"You can wait till the bank is closed to do that," Heather said.

"I know, but I'm so slow at this I thought I'd get a head start while we're not busy." I paused for a moment and then decided to plunge right in. "I came across something different a while ago," I said, hitting the enter key on my computer to activate the screen. "Look at all these figures flagged as 'dormant accounts.'" Heather's gaze darted to my screen. She quickly looked away with a seemingly uninterested shrug.

"I don't know anything about those accounts. Say, Cybil, you wouldn't have something for a headache, would you?"

I reached under the counter for my purse and took out a bottle of ibuprofen. "How many do you want?"

"Two, please."

I shook two pills into her palm.

"Thanks." She yawned hugely. "I don't know why I'm sleepy. I got nine hours last night."

She went back to her cage and tried to take the pills with swigs from her water bottle. From her expression I could tell she wasn't successful. I took a Dixie cup from my survival stash under the counter and handed her one.

She nodded her thanks. "I've always had trouble swallowing pills. I thought I'd outgrow the problem, but no such luck."

Nine hours of sleep. What a blessing. I envied her. Ever since my sweet little boy died, I had had trouble sleeping. I tried to dismiss the painful memory of Ryan, but I couldn't. All I managed to do was to shove it temporarily into a corner of my mind.

I turned back to my computer screen and stared at it for a while. As far as I knew, all tellers had access to all accounts. They had to, as they were obligated to help any customer who came to their window. So why would Heather claim to be unfamiliar with dormant accounts? From reading her personnel file I knew she'd been working at the bank for six years. How was it possible that in all that time she had never had to deal with a dormant account? According to the laws of probability, it wasn't possible. Why had she lied to me?

I pondered this until a customer claimed my attention.

Promptly at five, Heather asked, "Are you ready to go home?"

"Not yet, but you go ahead."

"Don't forget," she said, picking up her purse, "tomorrow it's our turn to fix lunch. I don't know if I mentioned it, but since Fridays are our long, busy days, we take turns bringing in lunch."

"The head teller told me," I said. "I'm bringing cookies, a pasta salad, and a tray of carrot and celery sticks. Should I also bring black olives?"

"Why not? All the women here love to eat. I'll pick up the tray of cheese and cold cuts I ordered at Kroger's and bring a loaf of bread."

"Then we're all set."

"I'm going to change out of this ugly uniform," she said with a grimace of distaste. She headed for the women's locker room.

The Westport National Bank was one of the few banking institutions around that made its tellers wear uniforms. They weren't really uniforms. The female tellers wore black skirts and white blouses and the men khaki pants and white shirts. I didn't think the outfits were ugly. Besides, the uniform did away with the annoying question each morning of what to wear.

When Heather returned, I was counting the last stack of money. She had changed into a clingy black jersey dress that hugged the generous curves of her figure. The chunky gold earrings and heavy chain she wore looked more expensive than any jewelry I owned.

"You look great," I said.

"Thanks." She reached down to brush something from her right shoe.

I did a double take. She was wearing a pair of Ferragamo pumps I'd coveted until I'd seen the price tag. "Going somewhere special?"

She smiled. "I have a dinner date."

Judging by her expression, I figured the man she was meeting had to be special. I felt a smidgeon of envy. Not that I was never asked out to dinner, but it was usually by my estranged husband. And not that Luke wasn't attractive or sexy. He was, but things were still sort of tense between us, so I kept turning him down.

That meant that I usually dined alone on such delicacies as peanut butter sandwiches and canned soup—unless my grandmother took pity on me and brought me one of her Austrian-Hungarian specialties. My favorites were chicken and dumplings and stuffed cabbage with dark rye bread. Fortunately for me, Maxi liked to cook and liked my company, so I got at least a couple of good meals a week.

From the window I watched Heather drive off in a BMW. The gold jewelry could be an heirloom and so be legitimate, but owning sinfully expensive shoes and a late model, top-of-the-line luxury car on a teller's salary? No way. Heather's financial record would be among the first I'd take a look at.

The next day, Heather didn't show up for work. All morning I waited for her to arrive but she didn't. Nor did she call in sick. I was getting alarmed. Not about Heather, I'm ashamed to confess, because I suspected she was with the man who'd taken her out to dinner—but about the fact that without her food, there wouldn't be enough for lunch.

During my coffee break I grabbed my purse and dashed to the only convenience-cum-grocery store in downtown Victoria Grove. *Downtown* was a seriously misleading term, as the area consisted of three short blocks, but as the natives called it that, I thought of it that way too. I bought ham and American cheese, a loaf of white bread, and a small jar of mayonnaise.

Back at the bank I set out the food in the staff break room. Before I returned to my station, I dialed Heather's phone number for the third time. I got the answering machine again.

The bank didn't close, so the tellers had staggered lunch breaks. I took the last one, and because of a chatty customer, I was late. All that was left of my pasta salad were a couple of grape tomatoes in the bottom of the bowl. I settled for some ham and cheese and a few carrot sticks.

I joined Clark Bailey, the branch manager, who stood by the window, finishing his sandwich.

"Does Heather Atkins have a history of not calling in when she's going to be absent?" I asked without preamble.

His bright blue eyes widened in surprise. "She didn't call in? That's not like her. She's got the best attendance record in the whole bank. She and Edward take turns earning the employee-of-the-month award."

Edward was the head teller, a good-looking guy in his mid-fifties but with a nervous mannerism that was most distracting. In moments of stress and unease—at least I assumed it was in those moments—he simultaneously lifted his left shoulder, squinted his left eye, and made a low throat-clearing noise. I truly didn't intend to mock him, but for some inexplicable reason I found myself reflexively wanting to squint and shrug in tandem with him. So, for obvious reasons, I avoided him. When that wasn't possible, I looked over his right shoulder.

"I think I'll stop at Heather's apartment on my way home to make sure she's okay," I said.

"You've been there?" Clark asked.

"No. She told me she lived in the small apartment complex on Maple Street. I drive past it on my way to Westport."

He nodded. "Her apartment's upstairs, at the east end of the building."

Not much had been done to disguise the fact that the Oak Tree apartment complex had originally been a two-story motel. The apartments all opened on a long concrete walkway on the ground floor and on a long, narrow wooden porch on the floor above.

It wasn't until I climbed the stairs to Heather's apartment that I wondered how Clark Bailey had known exactly where Heather lived. A workplace romance? I had a hard time picturing the pleasure-loving, mid-twenties blond being involved with a married man more than twice her age. There was little future in such a relationship, and Heather struck me as a woman very much interested in her future.

I knocked on the door of Heather's apartment. I could hear noises. I knocked again. Still no answer. I pressed my ear against the door. I could hear different voices and laughter. The television. Most likely a game show. I knocked harder, longer, but there was no response.

The uneasy feeling that gripped me drove me downstairs to the door marked MANAGER. The woman must have been watching me because she jerked the door open before I could knock.

"Could you please unlock Heather Atkins's door for me?"

"Who're you?" she asked, then crammed a handful of potato chips into her mouth from the bag clutched to her skinny chest.

"My name is Cybil Quindt. I work with Heather. She didn't come to work today and she didn't call in."

"Maybe she ain't up there."

"The television's on."

The woman shrugged, giving me a so-what look.

"What if she's had an accident? What if she's sick? By refusing to check on her, you're leaving yourself wide open to a lawsuit." I was bluffing. I had no idea if she would be liable, but I was counting on the fact that nobody liked to be sued.

"I'll get the key," she muttered crossly.

Even though I was seething with impatience and full of dark premonitions, I adjusted my steps to match her unhurried pace. Before we started up the stairs, she paused, fished the last bits and pieces of chips from the bottom of the bag, and tossed them into her mouth. I bit my tongue to keep from urging her to hurry.

When she finally unlocked the door, I pushed past her and then wished I hadn't. Heather lay sprawled on the couch, her eyes open but unseeing.

"She asleep?" the manager asked, looking over my shoulder.

I had to swallow before I could answer. "I don't think so." To make sure, I checked Heather's pulse. There was none. Her skin felt cold.

"Call nine-one-one," I told the woman.

"Is she dead?"

"I'm afraid so."

"Jeez. I'm gonna be sick."

"No, you're not," I said, turning the woman by her shoulder and walking her out the door. "Make the call." I closed the door behind her and then leaned against it. Even though I'd worked for my uncle for several months and I'd found a couple of dead bodies, my knees felt weak, my hands were shaky, and my mouth was dry.

I had also worked at the agency long enough to know

that Uncle Barney would expect a report. I looked around but didn't touch anything.

Heather had kicked off her beautiful shoes but otherwise she was dressed as she'd been when I last saw her, down to the expensive gold jewelry. So it hadn't been a robbery. Startled, I wondered why I assumed that this wasn't a natural death. Before I could pursue this thought, I heard the police sirens.

The next morning I went to the agency dressed casually in jeans and a T-shirt. Uncle Barney was waiting for me in his office. Two mugs of strong, black coffee sat on his desk. He pushed one toward me.

"Could you sleep last night, after the sheriff got through with you?" he asked.

"Eventually. For a few hours." I picked up the mug and took a sip of coffee. Lynn Nguyen, the office manager and petite tyrant, made good coffee.

"Tell me everything again," Uncle Barney said. "Lynn can take notes." He motioned to Lynn, who, as usual, hovered just outside the door.

I liked the idea of Lynn taking notes because it would save me from having to write a report. Lynn had taken off her suit jacket, her idea of dressing down on Saturdays. I might have imagined the disapproving look in her almond-shaped black eyes as she glanced at my jeans, but I didn't think so. I saw nothing wrong with my jeans. They were clean. I had even ironed them.

Collecting my thoughts, I reported the facts succinctly. With client interviews Uncle Barney liked verbatim reports but with events, he wanted summaries.

"Give me your impression of the scene you found when you opened the door," he said, fiddling with his unlit pipe.

"It looked to me as if Heather had invited her date, or someone, to come up and have a drink. There was a bottle of Tanqueray gin and an empty bottle of tonic water on the coffee table. One glass, sort of squat, sat on the table, untouched. From its position I'd say it belonged to the visitor. The other lay on the rug, near Heather's hand, as if she'd dropped it. The ice bucket contained a couple of inches of water. From the melted ice, I assume. The television was on."

"Were there any signs of a struggle? Furniture turned over, ashtrays spilled, stuff like that?"

Mentally I revisited the room. I shook my head. "No. She looked as if she'd fallen asleep. Or passed out. I don't suppose we'll find out what the autopsy report says today?"

"I'll call Sam on Monday."

Sam Keller, Uncle Barney's nephew and my cousin, was a detective with the Westport police department, which was really lucky for us as it saved us lots of red tape. I got up and paced the floor. "I can't believe Heather just died. She was only twenty-six. That's three years younger than me."

"It happens sometimes," Uncle Barney said. "We'll

wait for the results of the autopsy report. In the meantime, go back to the bank on Monday. Our assignment isn't finished."

I headed for my office and then stopped. "Do you suppose there's a connection between the embezzling and her death?"

"Too early to speculate. Let's wait for the report."

Although Uncle Barney believed in hunches and never ridiculed my leaps of intuition, he didn't indulge in fanciful speculation. At least not out loud. I waited until Lynn had typed the report. Then I signed it and went home.

During my morning break on Monday I phoned Uncle Barney. He hadn't heard anything from Sam and didn't until Wednesday morning.

"Heather's death has been ruled a suicide," he told me. "She mixed alcohol and drugs."

"A suicide? I don't believe that."

"Cybil, is that a gut reaction or do you know something concrete?"

"It's a gut reaction," I admitted, feeling a little deflated. "But she was so eager for life. She loved pretty clothes, going out to dinner, being admired by men. Heather was about as far from being depressed as you can get. Why would she take her life?"

Uncle Barney was quiet for so long that I suspected he remembered the deep depression I'd sunk into after Ryan's death. Since going back to work as a social worker or guidance counselor had seemed impossible, he had offered me the apprenticeship in an attempt to keep me busy and out of the clutches of despair. I'm sure my grandmother had suggested this.

Finally, he said, "Maybe it was an accident. Maybe she took the wrong pill. We'll know more after the toxicology report is in."

"When will that be?"

"A couple of weeks. Maybe longer."

Trying to maintain a professional demeanor, I suppressed a groan of frustration. "I'll report in tomorrow," I said and hung up.

An hour later I was summoned to the bank manager's office, where Joan Bower waited for me.

"Heather had no family," Joan said. "She named the bank as the executor of her estate."

"Is there an estate?"

"Probably not much of one, but I want you to go to her apartment and make an inventory. The police are finished there."

I was about to question this request when it occurred to me that Joan had a motive for asking me. If Heather had been responsible for embezzling from the dormant accounts, I might find evidence of that in the apartment.

"Okay," I said, "but with Heather gone, we're short-handed."

"I'm sending a teller from the main branch. How long will it take to do the inventory?" Joan asked.

"It's a small apartment. Probably three or four hours."

"Can you start in the morning?"

"Yes."

Driving past Heather's apartment on the way home, I made an illegal U-turn. I had nothing planned for the evening, so why not do the inventory now?

I stopped at the manager's office and asked for the key. The woman still eyed me suspiciously but gave it to me.

As soon as I entered Heather's apartment, my scalp tightened in apprehension. Something wasn't right. Then I smelled it: cigarette smoke. Not the stale smell of smoke lingering in curtains, rugs, or furniture, but the smell of a cigarette just lit.

The drapes were drawn, making the apartment dusky. Waiting for my eyes to adjust, I stood still and listened intently. I thought I heard a stealthy movement in the next room. I snatched my car keys from my pocket and looked for the pepper spray. Blast. I'd had to take it off at the airport on my last trip and had forgotten to put it back on the chain. Uncle Barney wouldn't let me get a gun permit until my apprenticeship was completed. I understood his reasoning, but it left me defenseless. Of course, he also reasoned that I wasn't supposed to get into a situation where I needed a gun.

I glanced around for something to use as a weapon. I saw a heavy ceramic bowl. I picked it up.

The living room was separated from the kitchen by a pair of swinging doors. Just as I reached for them, they were swung forward forcefully from the other side—so forcefully that they knocked me backward. I staggered and went down. I felt more than saw a figure rushing past me, all pants legs and sneakers. By the time I got up and limped to the door, the intruder was gone. I scanned the parking lot but saw no one. A minute later I heard a car start on the street and drive off, tires screeching. The intruder had parked on the street. Blast again. I had hoped to get a look at the car since I hadn't had a look at him. Or her.

Disgruntled, I went back into the apartment and locked the door behind me. After turning on the light, I looked at the room. I couldn't tell if the intruder had searched it or not, but I would. I pulled a pair of latex gloves from my purse, slipped my hands into them, and started. I'd search the perimeter and then go down the middle, the way Uncle Barney had taught me.

I searched the couch, feeling a momentary twinge when I remembered seeing Heather's body on it. I practically took it apart, but my search netted only a dime, three pennies, a hairpin, and a paper clip. I found nothing interesting until I searched the armchair in which Heather's visitor had perhaps sat on the night of her death.

The fabric beneath the seat cushion was ripped. The slight lump I felt turned out to be a big capsule. Staring at it, my first thought was that it couldn't belong to

Heather, who'd had trouble taking the much smaller ibuprofen tablets. There was no way she could swallow this huge pill. Did it belong to her visitor? I wondered what it was. I knew just the man to ask.

I phoned the ER and asked for Luke. I always felt guilty doing this, as I knew my husband had left orders that I be put through to him whenever I called except when he was in the middle of a crisis.

"Luke, I'm sorry to bother you, but I'll take only a moment of your time," I said in a rush.

"Take several moments, Cybil. I wish you would."

Luke had a low, sexy voice, especially on the phone. Or in the dark, murmuring sweet words. His voice still got to me no matter how much I steeled myself against it. My throat felt a little tight, but I ignored it.

"I found a pill. Actually, it's a capsule. If I describe it, can you tell me what it is?"

"I can try. Cybil, I thought your uncle put you into a nice safe bank. What are you doing with a mystery capsule?"

"I *am* working in a nice safe bank," I said, my voice defensive. Luke could put me on the defensive faster than anyone I knew, and I resented it. "This is what the capsule looks like." I described it before he could say anything else or ask more questions.

"I'd have to see it before I'd testify in court what it is, but I'm fairly sure it's Nembutal. It's a sleeping pill. Cybil, I know you have trouble sleeping, but you're not taking something not prescribed by your doctor?"

"Of course not. Luke, I've been married to you long enough not to do something that stupid."

"It's good to know you remember that we're married."

"Luke, let's not get into that right now. Thanks for your help." I hung up before he could say anything else. I knew my husband. If I hadn't hung up, he'd have urged me not to get mixed up in other people's business or asked me out to dinner. Maybe both, and we hadn't resolved any of our differences. Sometimes I wondered if we ever would. Or could.

I placed the capsule into one of the small plastic bags I carried in my purse and put it into my pocket. I went back to my search. Heather's kitchen yielded nothing of interest except that she had cooked even less often than I. She didn't even have staples in her cupboard except instant coffee and pink packets of sweetener.

Her bedroom was lots more interesting, at least as far as her expensive clothes were concerned. Her lingerie drawer amazed me. Comparing it with mine, I came up with the short end of the stick. The most recent under-wear I remembered buying was the kind that came three to a pack and was not only washable in hot water, but you could also bleach the hell out of it.

I didn't find anything significant until I tore the bed apart. When I examined the pillow inch by inch, I felt something hard. I didn't relish digging through a bunch of smelly feathers, so I worked the object to the edge of the seam. Using Heather's nail scissors, I ripped the stitches. The object turned out to be a man's cuff link with the initials S.R. engraved in the heavy gold.

I stared at the ornate, expensive cuff link for a long time. Why sew it inside a pillow? To keep it safe? Was it a sentimental keepsake? The pillow also made a good hiding place, but again, why hide it? True, the cuff link was expensive, but it wouldn't be worth anything in a pawn shop unless Heather had the set. Blackmail? An ugly idea but not out of the realm of possibilities.

Whatever Heather's reasons had been, the cuff link had obviously been important to her. I placed it into another plastic bag and shoved it deep into my skirt pocket.

Suddenly I was tired. I would enter the contents of the bedroom in my report tomorrow.

Maxi had phoned that she'd put a casserole into my empty refrigerator. I could hardly wait to get home and sample it.

It had grown dark outside, and the light bulb over the stairs was out. I could picture the sour, resentful expression on the manager's face when I'd ask her to replace it. I'd probably have to mention lawsuits again to get any action. I smiled as I walked down the steps.

At the bottom of the stairs someone grabbed me from behind. I opened my mouth to yell, but a cloth pressed over my face cut off my scream. I struggled, but the sickening smell of ether dragged me relentlessly into a bottomless darkness.

Chapter Two

I gasped when the cold water hit my body. I opened my mouth to yell in protest, only to swallow water, inhale it into my nose, feel it press against my chest, feel it suck me into its inky depth. Instinctively, wildly, I kicked my legs and flailed my arms to escape, to reach life-giving air.

Just as I thought my lungs would explode, I broke through to the surface. I gasped in air greedily. When my panic subsided and my breathing became less labored, I became aware of the sound of a motor. I looked around. Maybe ten feet away a boat idled in the water, a light from it sweeping over the area around it.

Help was near. I wouldn't die. I raised my arm and opened my mouth to hail the boat when something about the whole situation hit me as being wrong. The ether had left me still a little groggy, so my thinking wasn't clear. The light turned slowly in my direction. Acting strictly on instinct, I let myself sink under the water.

Using the breaststroke, which I knew wouldn't cause ripples on the surface, I swam away from the boat. I stayed under as long as I could hold my breath. Then I surfaced cautiously, quietly.

The cold water had helped clear my head, and I now realized the source of my instinctive unease. I hadn't driven myself to this lake. I hadn't jumped into the water. Whoever was on that boat had brought me here and had tossed me into the water like an undersized fish not worth keeping.

I had more than doubled my distance from the boat, but it still seemed too close. The light beam now searched the water to the left of me. The person on board was waiting to make sure I had drowned. Any moment, it could swing back in my direction. I took another deep breath and dove under the water again.

Whoever was on that boat didn't know that my sport of choice in high school had been swimming and that I still swam laps at the YWCA pool at least three times a week. That evened the odds between me and the killer on the boat. Fueled by this knowledge, I made every stroke as precise and efficient as if I were at a swim meet.

When I resurfaced, I wondered if I was far enough from the boat to risk swimming on the surface. Maybe, but in which direction? Where was I? Lake Michigan? For an instant my heartbeat accelerated into panic mode. No. This couldn't be the big lake. For one thing, the water was neither cold nor choppy enough. For another, I could see lights all around me. On Lake Michigan I might see lights to the east and possibly to the south, but not all around. This had to be one of the smaller lakes near Westport.

My mood took an upswing. I could make it to the shore, if the person on the boat didn't spot me and run me down. Once again I dove under the water and swam toward the nearest lights on land. When I emerged, I saw the boat turn and head in my direction. Had I been spotted?

Taking a hasty breath, I let myself sink and stayed under until my chest threatened to burst. I came up gasping for air.

The boat had passed me and was headed for shore. Unfortunately, it was also heading in the direction of the nearest land. Since I hadn't seen the person who'd pressed the ether-soaked cloth over my mouth and dumped me unceremoniously into the lake, I couldn't risk crawling out of the water and straight into his or her murderous grasp. That left the opposite shore, which was a good bit farther away, but I had no choice.

This was going to be just like another swim competition, I told myself. I can do this. I started out with an easy, measured crawl. Though I paced myself, the distance to the north shore was considerable and my full skirt seemed to weigh a ton. I had lost my high-heeled pumps in the water. Briefly I considered struggling out of my skirt, but didn't relish wading ashore clad in nothing but my underwear.

When my strength flagged, I flipped onto my back and floated for a while. However, the spring air was cool and forced me all too soon to resume swimming.

By the time I dragged myself ashore, I was cold, exhausted, and nauseated. The latter was probably due to the ether. Before I had walked half a dozen steps I had to run into the bushes to throw up. Then I sank into the grass, weak and shaky. The guy with the ether was going to pay for this dearly. I would have liked to rest longer, but I was rapidly getting chilled and shivered like a wet dog. I couldn't risk my body getting stiff.

The first four houses I tried were apparently weekend homes and empty on a Monday night. The woman who came to the door at the fifth house gasped and yelled for her husband to come quickly.

"I know I look awful," I said, feeling like the Creature from the Black Lagoon, "but I fell off a boat. Could you make a phone call for me? Collect? Please?" My teeth were chattering so hard I could hardly utter the words.

The husband took one look at me and asked, "The boat you fell off didn't stop to pick you up?"

Oh, the boat had stopped all right, but not to pick me up. Aloud I said, "Please call my uncle. He'll come and get me." I gave them Uncle Barney's cell phone number.

The man repeated it and dashed back inside.

I hugged my arms around myself, trying to get warm. The woman handed me a towel to dry my face and arms.

"Your uncle will be here shortly," the man reported. "Why don't you come in?"

I saw the alarmed look his wife shot him. "Thanks, but I'm dripping all over. I'll ruin your floor. I'll wait out front."

"At least take another towel," the woman said, "and this beach blanket."

"Thanks." I used the towel to blot my hair and the blanket to wrap around myself.

"You need medical attention," Uncle Barney said.

"No, there's no need for that. Just take me home, please. All I need is a hot shower and a good night's sleep."

Uncle Barney was too dignified a man to snort, but I sensed he wanted to.

"Okay," he agreed after one of his characteristic silences. "But I'm phoning Luke and asking him to come to your place and take a look at you."

I groaned loudly.

"It's Luke or the hospital. Which will it be?"

"Luke," I said, though I didn't look forward to my husband's censorious looks and comments. I wrapped the blanket Uncle Barney had brought tighter around myself as I half listened to his brief phone conversation with my husband.

At my house I went straight to the shower, where I stood under the hot water until I stopped shivering. I shampooed my hair and scrubbed the lake water from my skin. I couldn't remember whether Three Finger Lake was unpolluted enough to allow swimming. Not that it mattered. It was too late to worry about being exposed to polluted water.

When I finished, I found Luke in the living room, leaning against the fireplace, waiting for me. He looked deceptively relaxed with his hands in the pockets of his khaki pants, but I wasn't fooled. His perceptive dark eyes took in every aspect of my appearance. I tightened the belt of my terry robe.

While Luke listened to my heart and lungs, Uncle Barney asked questions.

"Let's go over this one more time. Think, Cybil. What can you tell me about the man who grabbed you at the bottom of the stairs? I think we can safely assume it was a man."

"I'm sure it was a man because he held me with one arm so tightly pressed around my chest that I couldn't even struggle effectively. And his hand was big enough to cover most of my face. At least that's what it felt like." I had half expected to get a lecture on not carrying the pepper spray in my hand ready to use, but Uncle Barney must have thought I'd been through enough for one night. I suspected I'd get that lecture at another time.

"Anything at all you noticed about him?"

I shrugged apologetically. "It happened so fast. Except he had eaten something with cinnamon. I remember smelling cinnamon."

"Anything else?"

"No. I think it took only seconds for me to pass out from the ether." That got Luke's attention.

"Ether? How come I'm only now hearing about it?" he demanded with an accusing look at Uncle Barney.

I intervened quickly. "I'm okay. I threw up, but now I'm fine." I glanced all around the room, but carefully avoided Luke's eyes.

He lifted my chin with his hand, forcing me to look at him. "You're okay? Really? Then you'll be ready for some food. How about some ham hocks, big dumplings—"

"Please," I pleaded, "don't." The thought of heavy food, any food, made my stomach heave in protest.

"So you're still nauseated."

It wasn't a question. Why was I so bad at trying to keep something from Luke? We'd been married for seven years and separated for one and still I couldn't fool him.

Luke had come prepared. I watched him take a bottle of pills from his medical bag and put one into the palm of my hand.

"Uncle Barney, will you get a glass of water for Cybil?"

"Sure thing."

"What's the pill for?" I asked, eyeing him warily.

"Your nausea."

I got up from the sofa. "Speaking of pills," I said, and retrieved the bag with the capsule from the pocket of my wet skirt. "I didn't lose it and it didn't dissolve," I said, relieved.

"The plastic protected it." Luke looked at the capsule. "Is this the Nembutal you asked me about earlier?"

"Yes." Uncle Barney came back with the water and I took the nausea pill. "The sheriff claims that Heather killed herself. I don't believe it. Luke, does it seem possible that a woman who had trouble swallowing a pill as little as an ibuprofen could swallow a bunch of these capsules?"

"It's not impossible, but unlikely."

"Uncle Barney, what do you think?"

"As Luke said, it seems unlikely."

"These capsules can be opened and their content poured into a drink?" I asked.

Luke nodded.

"If the drink is gin and tonic, would the bitter flavor of the tonic disguise the drug's taste?"

Both men thought that it would.

"What are you getting at?" Luke asked.

"That Heather didn't kill herself," I said. "Whoever her visitor was put the Nembutal into her drink."

"She could have emptied the sleeping pills into the drink herself," Luke pointed out.

"No. She didn't commit suicide. She wasn't the type."

"There's no *type*. All sorts of people kill themselves for all sorts of reasons," Luke said.

"But most of them are severely depressed, right?" I watched Luke nod reluctantly. "Heather wasn't. She was full of life and plans and excited about the man she was dating."

"I'm now leaning toward agreeing with Cybil," Uncle Barney said, tapping his unlit pipe against his chin. "The strongest argument against Heather committing suicide is tonight's attack on Cybil. Apparently Heather's killer thinks that Cybil saw or found something."

"But I haven't!" I exclaimed.

"You're going to report the attack to the police," Luke said, his tone commanding.

"No! Absolutely not," I said.

For a moment Luke looked merely confused and then angry. "Why not? It was attempted murder."

"It's up to Cybil to report it if she wishes," Uncle Barney said.

I shook my head. "I'd have to report it to the sheriff since it happened in the county. He didn't impress me when he ruled Heather's death a suicide. You have to remember that his is an elected office. He's not a trained investigator."

"I think you don't want to report it because you want to investigate it yourself," Luke said accusingly.

"The agency will investigate," Uncle Barney said, his

voice firm. "Cybil's job is in the bank, watching dormant accounts. That's what we were hired for."

"You heard that, right?" Luke asked me pointedly.

The look I flicked at him wasn't exactly friendly.

"Cybil?" Luke asked, obviously waiting for my confirmation.

"Yes, I heard. I'm reporting to the bank as usual." Then I tapped my hand against my forehead, remembering. "Wait a minute." I hurried into the bathroom and retrieved the other plastic bag. I took out the cuff link and held it out to Uncle Barney, who took it and studied it carefully.

"Expensive. Probably custom designed," he said. "Where did you find it?"

"Inside a pillow on Heather's bed. And no, it couldn't have gotten there by accident. The scam was sewn shut. The cuff link was hidden." I yawned hugely.

Luke faced Uncle Barney with an accusatory expression. "I thought you said you'd put Cybil into a *quiet, staid* bank. Those were your very words!"

"I did put her into such a bank. It doesn't get any more quiet or staid than the Victoria Grove branch bank."

Luke turned to me, his dark eyes intense, his hands braced against his trim waist. "I swear, Cybil, only you could find trouble in a bank."

"I wasn't looking for trouble," I protested. "Honestly." I yawned again. Briefly I considered telling both of them to back off and let me make my own decisions. However, I knew from past experience that letting them think I was going along with their recommendations and then doing my own thing was a lot easier. I had done that in the past and would do it again in the future. Right now I was also too tired to fight with them.

"You're staying home tomorrow. Don't argue," Luke said with the considerable authority of a man who ran the emergency service at the hospital. "It wouldn't surprise me if you came down with a cold, or pneumonia or gastritis. That lake isn't known for its pure water."

"I'll call the bank in the morning and report that you're sick," Uncle Barney offered.

I yawned again. "Why am I so sleepy?" Then it dawned on me. "What else was in that pill you gave me?"

Luke shrugged. "It has a mild sedative effect on some people," he admitted.

His voice and expression were seemingly innocent, but I knew my husband. "A mild sedative effect on *some* people? I bet on all, you stinker. I need to think about this case. Discuss it with Uncle Barney . . ." Another yawn stopped me. By now my eyelids felt like steel shutters.

Without a word, Luke swept me up in his arms and carried me to my bed.

The ringing of the phone woke me the next morning. Glancing at my bedside clock, I muttered, "Who'd call me at five?"

It turned out it was no one. At least no one spoke when I picked up the receiver. Wrong number. I snuggled back under the covers.

The next thing I became aware of was Luke sitting on my bed, checking my pulse. My grandmother was hovering beside him.

"How do you feel, *Schatzi*?" she asked.

"Oma. What are you doing here?"

"Taking care of you," Luke told me.

"I can take care of myself."

"Yeah, right," Luke muttered, giving me a dark look. "That's why you got yourself anesthetized and tossed into a lake. How much longer are you going to persist in this lunacy you call your new career?"

"It's not lunacy. Why can't you give me credit that I'm actually not half bad at this job?" Then, recalling that I had gotten dumped into a lake, I backpedaled. "I *am* getting better with experience." Then I noticed that he was wearing the same shirt. "Did you stay here all night?"

"Yes."

His expression dared me to object. I didn't. I rather liked the fact that he'd stayed. He hadn't shaved, which gave him a slightly disreputable look. I remembered that look well from the days when we were first married and he was an intern at the hospital. He'd dash home between shifts for a change of clothes, a quick meal, and—

"I'm going to fix breakfast," Maxi said hastily, trying

to break the tension around us. "Luke, you'll stay for blueberry pancakes, won't you?"

"He has to go to the hospital," I said, not too graciously.

"I have time for breakfast. Thanks," he said and beamed a smile at Maxi.

Luke liked my grandmother, and she adored him. As soon as Maxi left, I said, "Luke, why did you phone Maxi? I'm perfectly all right—"

"Maxi would never forgive me if I hadn't called her. Let her take care of you. Now take a deep breath."

I flinched when I felt the cold stethoscope against my skin. "There was a time when you warmed the stethoscope with your hands," I grumbled.

"There was a time when I did many things."

That shut me up.

During my absence from the bank, Mr. Bailey had made the funeral arrangements for Heather. I was grateful he hadn't asked me to help, as I had a hard time with funerals and cemeteries.

Westport had two burial grounds. Fortunately for me, Heather wasn't going to be interred in the one where my little boy lay at rest. I still couldn't go to his grave without falling apart.

At Klowitter's Funeral Home I looked unobtrusively at the cards attached to the flower arrangements, wondering if Heather's special man had sent one. I suspected that the bouquet of red roses with baby's breath, identified only by a generic Teleflora sympathy card, was his. I removed the card when no one seemed to be watching and put it into my handbag. Uncle Barney would undoubtedly assign one of the operatives to trace the sender.

The funeral triggered only a minor panic attack, which I fought by sitting in my car until I stopped shaking and could breathe normally. Maybe I was making some progress in overcoming these attacks.

After the brief graveside service, Mr. Bailey hosted a reception at his home. I accepted a glass of orange juice and stood by the bay window, observing my fellow bank employees.

"Good turnout," Edward said, limping over to join me.

I noticed that at times his limp was more pronounced than at other times. I wondered idly what had caused the injury to his leg, but couldn't think of a tactful way to ask. "It's nice of Mr. Bailey to do this."

"Well, it's the least he can do. If you take my meaning."

I risked looking at him, hoping he wouldn't be hit with one of his squinting-shrugging-throat-clearing mannerisms. He wasn't. "I don't know what you mean," I said. "Remember, I'm new to the bank."

"Well, when Heather first joined us, she and Mr. Bailey were like this." Edward placed his middle finger over his index finger, implying extreme closeness.

I didn't like his smug expression. Ordinarily, I would have walked away, but I sensed he was a willing source of information. And gossip. "Do you know the man she was dating lately?"

"No. She kept him secret. Except to imply he had lots of money and didn't mind spending it on her."

I perceived a trace of bitterness in the head teller's voice. Had he been Heather's unsuccessful suitor? Unlikely. I had a hard time seeing Edward as an ardent beau. He seemed too prissy, too fussy, too old-maidenish for the emotionally untidy game of pursuit, conquest, and love. Maybe he was merely protective of the women he supervised.

"I think he's a married man," Edward added.

"What makes you think that?"

"Why else keep him such a secret? She never did that with her other boyfriends."

"She had others?" Edward's chuckle at my question was of the snide variety.

"Oh, yes. Our Heather was never short of boyfriends. How do you think she got that expensive wardrobe and jewelry?"

By accessing dormant accounts? I barely stopped myself from blurting that out. "You didn't like Heather?"

"I didn't say that."

"But?"

"I was a little disappointed in her. When she first came to us, I thought she'd go far. I encouraged her to take evening classes at the university. I thought she might take my place as head teller when I retired."

A disappointed mentor. Perhaps not so very different from a disappointed suitor. "She wasn't interested in advancing her career?"

"More interested in men. Men with money."

The bitterness was back in Edward's voice and his squinting-shrugging-throat clearing mannerism soared into full force. I was careful not to look straight at him. I was sure the poor man couldn't control this nervous habit that drove me crazy.

Edward had also given himself a motive for Heather's murder. What if he was the one embezzling money from the dormant accounts? He might have thought that if he had ready cash Heather might get interested in him. As Maxi never tired of saying, the human heart had an inexhaustible capacity for self-deception. What if Heather caught him and threatened to expose him? No, from what I'd learned about her, she'd be more apt to blackmail him. The result would be the same: he would feel cornered, threatened. Edward definitely merited a closer look.

Carol, who worked two cages down from me, walked by and nodded to us. I noticed that her upper lip was split and one side of her face looked puffy.

"Now there's a pitiful case," Edward said.

"Carol? Why do you say that?"

"You didn't notice how heavy her makeup was? Trying to cover the bruises her husband put on her face."

"He hits her?"

Edward rocked back on his heels. "Yup. Every time he gets drunk, which is once every other week and getting more often, I'm afraid."

Wife beaters, along with child abusers, were men I'd like to see locked up for the rest of their worthless, miserable lives. Along with rapists, of course. These lousy excuses for men inflicted pain and often irreparable damage on those weaker than them. How much guts did it take to do that?

"Why does he beat her?" I couldn't stop myself from asking.

Edward shrugged. "Claims she's holding out money on him to keep him from drinking."

"He expects her to give him drinking money?"

"Well, yes, since he can't hold down a job."

Right then and there I made up my mind to speak to Carol, to tell her that she had options, that she didn't have to be some creep's punching bag. We had shelters and women's groups who could help her. I knew the women who ran them from my time as a social worker.

Of course, Carol now also had a motive for embezzling. If she brought more money home, her worthless husband might not beat her.

If my speculations were correct, how had Heather discovered Carol's embezzling? Tellers were not allowed to transact their personal banking. They had to let one of the other tellers handle their deposits and withdrawals. However, since Joan Bower had shown me how to access dormant accounts, probably any bright teller could figure out how to do it. Although the tellers worked next to each other, separated only by waist-high partitions, it was not possible to watch each other closely, especially during the busy parts of the day.

Edward motioned to Agnes Miller to join us. The assistant head teller, a quiet if not downright dour woman, had not said anything to me the entire time I'd been at the bank except hello and goodbye. Looking at her closely for the first time, I discovered that she could be a nice-looking woman if she applied a bit of make-up to lend color to her sallow complexion. And let her short-cropped hair curl around her face instead of slicking it back so severely.

"Excuse me," Edward said to me, "Agnes and I have to discuss a little bank business now that we're short-handed."

I nodded that I understood and walked away. I stopped to speak to a couple of tellers before I found our host and thanked him for inviting me.

On my way home, I detoured to Heather's apartment. For a moment I hesitated, remembering that this was the site of the recent attack on me. The ether. Every time I thought about it, I felt queasy.

I had a key now but hesitated before I unlocked the door. On a rational level I knew that there would be no dead body on the couch and enough time had passed that whatever the intruder had looked for, he had probably found. Pulling myself together, I entered the apartment.

What hadn't I looked at in detail the last time I was here? The papers in Heather's desk. Most of them turned out to be paid bills, but I found two things that were interesting. The first was a pamphlet on a Bible college in Michigan. Heather hadn't struck me as a religious woman, so why keep this information in her desk drawer? The other was a recurring phone number on her telephone bills. From the area code, I knew it was a Michigan number. I dialed it on my cell phone.

"Coach Inn. May I help you?"

I was momentarily startled. "Pardon me?"

The man's voice said, "This is the Coach Inn. How can I help you?"

"Where are you located?"

The desk clerk told me. I thanked him and hung up. Why did Heather repeatedly phone this motel in a small resort town on Lake Michigan? My instincts told me that this was a place I needed to visit. It was only about a ninety-minute drive from Heather's place.

I took a photo of her from the stack I found in the desk. It was a studio portrait, an excellent likeness. Her eyes seemed to look straight at me, full of joy and vitality. Whoever had robbed her of her life was going to pay.

The Coach Inn, with its sign depicting a coach drawn by six horses, looked inviting. It sat on a dune with a lovely view of the lake.

When I showed Heather's photo to the desk clerk, he smiled and nodded.

"That's Mrs. Jackson. She and her husband are regular guests."

Husband? "What's her husband's name?"

"Jeremy. I think they're scheduled to come this weekend."

I didn't have the heart to tell him that Heather would never come again. Needing a plausible reason to question him, I told him that I was doing this for the bank, a living trust, and an estate. This seemed to both sufficiently confuse and satisfy him.

"What does Mr. Jackson look like? You understand that we have to be sure we have the right couple before we contact them about the estate."

"He's probably in his mid-fifties, nice-looking, in good shape. Likes to sail and play golf. And he wears a rug."

I must have looked momentarily taken aback because he went on to explain.

"A toupee. An expensive one. It looks good."

"Ah. What kind of car does he drive?"

"A rental, so it's always a different one. But it was at least a mid-sized one, never an economy model."

"Any idea where they're from?"

The young man thought for a moment. "They never said, but I got the impression it was from the Detroit area."

I thanked him and left, feeling let down. I had expected this to be a hot clue, leading to Heather's killer. Instead the Coach Inn was merely the lovers' hideaway. Could her lover have turned into a murderer? At first I dismissed this as impossible. You don't kill the person you love. Or do you?

What if he had fallen out of love with Heather? What if he was, as Edward suggested, a married man? A married man whose wife suspected him of infidelity? From what I'd seen of cheating married men, they usually returned to their wives. They didn't usually want a divorce—just a little excitement on the side.

S.R., whoever he was, deserved a much closer scrutiny.

Chapter Three

Whistle I arrived at the bank the next morning and checked the dormant accounts I had flagged, I ground my teeth to keep the angry words from spilling out.

Turning to the teller on my left, I said, "Susan, I have to see Mr. Bailey for a minute. Can you handle things?"

Susan looked at the almost empty bank. She shrugged. "I guess so."

Her lack of enthusiasm wasn't lost on me, but I'd pegged her as a whiner days ago.

I hurried upstairs, where I found Mr. Bailey sitting behind his desk, drinking coffee.

"It's happened. Somebody accessed five of the dormant accounts I'd flagged."

"How much did the thief get?"

"Ten thousand dollars."

He swore so emphatically that his hand jerked, spilling coffee on his shirt. He swore again. Then he apologized for his language.

I grabbed some tissues from the box and handed them to him.

"Now that's brazen. Nobody's ever taken that much before," he said with grudging admiration.

"The thief's either brazen or desperate. I think it's time I did a financial check on all the tellers and asked them some tough questions."

"You're right. Start this morning."

"That'll leave us really short-handed downstairs. And what will I tell the women I work with?"

"You're a trainee. Time to work in a different department. Naturally, you'll keep an eye on the dormant accounts."

"Naturally." I thought for a moment. "Heather obviously wasn't the embezzler."

"Or not the only one."

"You think there could be more than one?"

"There could be. How strong was your case against Heather?" he asked.

I shrugged. "It was mostly circumstantial. She lived above her means."

"Lots of people do. That's why banks foreclose." He shrugged and paused to drink some coffee. "Heather was very good at . . . um . . . getting presents from her men friends."

His tone of voice, his choice of words, the slight hesitation, all hinted to me that these presents were perhaps not freely given. He looked a little embarrassed, suggesting that he, too, had been a coerced gift-giver. He probably suspected correctly that I'd heard the gossip about him and the young teller.

"How soon will you hire a replacement for Heather?"

"As soon as I find someone. I'll have to start interviews today."

He didn't look happy.

"Who runs your human resources department?"

"Since we're only a branch bank, the department is small. Actually, I'm in charge of it. With the help of Elaine. She does most of the grunt work." He suddenly perked up. "But as soon as your replacement arrives, you can do the preliminary interviews. You know, weed out the unsuitable candidates and send only the real possibilities to see me."

Mr. Bailey looked considerably happier after dumping this job into my lap. "All right," I agreed, not really having a choice. Since I'd worked as a guidance counselor during Luke's internship and residency, interviewing people wasn't terra incognita. At the door, I stopped. "I need to clean out Heather's locker for the new teller. Who has the combinations?"

"Elaine has them."

Elaine gave them to me without a question. I wasn't sure of my legal standing here. Hadn't there been a case before the courts where parents challenged the teachers' right to search student lockers? Except in my case the owner of the locker was beyond challenging me.

Heather's locker was crammed full. I had to take out the extra sets of clothes she kept there before I could get to the rest. It looked to me that Heather could change into a clean blouse and skirt if she didn't make it home after an all-night date. Nothing was more revealing of having slept over as wearing the same clothes two days in a row. She even kept a change of underwear and pantyhose in a plastic bag. She had been one well-organized woman.

I didn't know what it was about the makeup bag— the kind given out at cosmetic counters in department stores—that fairly called out to be searched. Under the false bottom I found a bracelet wrapped in tissue paper. Made of gold, it was studded with semi-precious stones. I took it to the window to read the words engraved on the underside. *To Heather with love. S.R.* At least this present didn't sound as if it had been given unwillingly.

After this discovery I examined every item with special care. Among a stack of photographs I found one of Heather wearing a bikini, reclining on the deck of a boat. By some trick of light and the position of the camera, the shadow of the photographer appeared in the snapshot. It was a man, judging by the size and build of the shadow. Behind Heather a round life preserver with the boat's name on it hung on the railing.

From my purse I took the tiny magnifying glass that I always carried and studied the circular tube. The name appeared to be *The Wolverine*. How could I find out details about the boat?

Then I remembered: Luke had taken up sailing in a big way. And whatever my husband did, he did with enthusiasm and thoroughness. He would know about boats. Now all I had to do was find the right moment to ask him.

I was sorting Heather's belongings into piles for disposal when I was interrupted by a knock on the door. Frowning, I wondered who it could be. None of the female employees knocked. As soon as I opened the door, Edward spoke.

"Could I come in? There's no one in here changing?"

Surprised by his request, I stepped aside to allow him to enter.

"So, you're cleaning out Heather's locker," he said, stating the obvious. "What are you going to do with her stuff?"

"Since she had no family, I'll take most of the items to Mercy Mission."

I watched him look at the various piles. Edward didn't try to disguise his curiosity. As I had put the bracelet and the photo into my purse, I saw no reason to stop him.

"What about the makeup stuff?"

"The shampoo, conditioner, and the liquid soap I'll take for the mission's shower room. They're always short of toiletries. People rarely think of donating these items." That was also true of underwear, though I didn't mention it. I knew this because I was on the board of the mission, and I worked there at least one Saturday a month. Years ago my role as a social worker had involved me with the mission, and I had never severed the connection.

Edward picked up the bottle of cologne and sniffed it. He touched the silk scarf and stared at the under-wear. This was making me a little uncomfortable. Was he a voyeur or just incurably nosy? That he was a bit of a gossip I'd found out on my first day at the bank. He must have become aware of my scrutiny, for he turned to the last pile of Heather's things.

"Photos! That's what I came in here for," he said, his voice hearty.

I had doubts about that but let it pass.

"We keep a scrapbook of the employees. Do you mind if I take a couple of photos?"

As I had looked through them and found none of them significant, I said, "You can take them all."

"Thanks," he said and walked out quickly.

Again I noticed that his limp didn't seem to bother him as much as it did at other times. Like Maxi's arthritis.

By mid-morning on Friday I had read every scrap of information on the tellers I could get my hands on, including their financial records. Now what? Talk to

Mr. Bailey or Joan Bower? I wasn't sure of the proper chain of command. Joan had hired the agency but Mr. Bailey was in charge of the bank. When in doubt, talk to Uncle Barney. He was my boss and the man I trusted implicitly.

I left the bank and headed for the agency. As always when I approached the building, I felt a surge of pleasure. The classical lines, the symmetry, the small Italianate touches around the windows were so visually pleasing.

Lynn, pointedly consulting her calendar, informed me that I didn't have an appointment to see Uncle Barney.

"Oh, for heaven's sake! I work here. I need to talk to him." I must have raised my voice, for Uncle Barney opened his door and motioned me inside. As I passed Lynn, I made the mistake of looking at her. Some time in the future I'd pay dearly in all sorts of small but aggravating inconveniences for this rash act of rebellion against her procedures. She insisted on personally announcing everyone to Uncle Barney. I didn't mind being announced. What I minded was the interrogation she subjected me to first.

Why Uncle Barney put up with this I could only speculate. And I confess I'd speculated plenty. I'd imagined everything from them meeting in Vietnam during the war and saving each other's lives, to him, being the kind man he was, feeling compassion for an immigrant, to them being lovers now or having been lovers in the past.

As I passed Lynn I thought I'd heard her hiss, but surely I was mistaken about that.

"I've read all the tellers' files," I said, sitting in the chair Uncle Barney indicated. "I looked at their financial records."

"You had permission to do that, I assume?" he asked.

"Yes. I'm not a snoop."

"I didn't mean to imply that you were. Just making sure our backs are covered legally. Go on."

"Agnes is the assistant head teller. She's single, but has no savings or assets, which is odd given the fact that she makes a decent salary."

Barney nodded. "Go on."

"Then there's Louise. She has one dependent and has a long history of taking out small loans. She repays them, but usually has to ask for an extension."

"Look into that."

"Of course. I already told you about Carol and her worthless, abusive, alcoholic husband. That leaves Susan. She works in the cage to my left and talks to me when we're not busy. Rather, she whines and complains, but she has reason to. They have a son who was born with a birth defect. He's had a number of operations, all expensive, none completely covered by insurance. I'm sure she would do most anything to get him the best care available." My voice had gotten softer and softer. I swallowed hard. I knew if my little boy had needed expensive medical treatments, I'd have done whatever it took to get them for him.

"That's rough." Uncle Barney walked to the window and opened it. He lit his pipe, something he usually did when he was thinking.

I sat quietly, waiting.

"So, all the tellers are in financial trouble except the head teller. What about him?"

"The only unusual thing I found about Edward was that he's made several large withdrawals from his savings account in the last six weeks. But he could have bought new appliances or paid for major repairs on his house or his car. Or maybe he's had medical bills. He limps a little. Like someone who had polio as a child. Or he could have been in an accident. Anyway, he's not in debt."

Uncle Barney continued to look out the window. "There are, of course, other motives for embezzling than financial difficulties," he said.

"Such as?" I asked.

"Blackmail. Revenge. The excitement of seeing if you can get away with it."

"That last one is odd."

"Some people like danger. They thrive on it."

"I must be a born coward then," I said. "I hate and fear danger."

"A normal, healthy reaction." He puffed on his pipe while I waited. "Of course, the embezzling may have nothing to do with Heather's death and the attack on you."

"I've thought about that too," I admitted with a sigh. "But why kill Heather? What reason could anyone have? She was good at her job. She was a lively, fun-loving young woman."

"That might be the reason. Too fun-loving with someone else's husband," Uncle Barney said.

I considered that for a bit. If some woman went after Luke, would I, could I, commit cold-blooded murder? Not cold-blooded. Definitely not cold-blooded. Not the way my heart rate sped up and anger coursed through my veins just thinking about it. I'd probably scratch the husband-stealing witch bald.

"Jealousy and betrayal are powerful emotions," he murmured.

Were they ever! I wasn't living with Luke by my own choice, and yet I was ready to commit mayhem on any woman who'd dare lay her hands on him. Bemused, I wondered what was wrong with me. Was this a case of "can't live with him, can't live without him"? Was I that much of an emotional mess? I sighed. This was no time to think about my relationship with Luke. I turned my attention back to business.

"We need to find out who S.R. is and if there's a Mrs. S.R. I wish we had some clues to his identity."

"But we have," Uncle Barney said. "We have the cuff link, which is custom designed. I'm assigning Glenn to start canvassing jewelers in the area as he has time."

"I'll help. I'll check the jewelery stores in Westport. The clerk at the motel said he thought the couple came from the Detroit area."

"Then we'll canvass Detroit too."

"That's going to run into money. The bank only hired us to investigate the embezzling, not murder."

"When someone attempts to kill one of my people, I take it personally. No one does that to my favorite niece and gets away with it."

It took a second before I realized that I was the one he was talking about. A lump settled in my throat.

He took my hand and squeezed it. "Are you ready for the Mother's Day cookout on your grandmother's farm?"

"I haven't thought about it." That wasn't strictly true. I had thought about it but hadn't made a decision. Last Mother's Day my little boy had made a card for me with Luke's help. He'd been so proud of the card and had explained it so earnestly. He'd chosen purple construction paper because that was my favorite color. He'd made the tulips pink because he'd helped me plant pink tulips in the fall, and the many Xs were the hugs and kisses I loved to get from him. I felt a pain in my chest, heavy, crushing, that made breathing difficult.

"Shall I come and pick you up?" Uncle Barney asked.

"You're afraid I'll chicken out, aren't you?"

"Will you?" Uncle Barney asked gently.

"I don't know. I don't know if I can come," I admitted.

"It won't be easy, but won't it be easier than staying at home alone, remembering? On the farm you'll be surrounded by people who love and care about you. Your mother will be there. And your grandmother will be so disappointed if you don't come. She'll worry about you the whole time."

"That's emotional blackmail," I protested.

"I know. I didn't mean to do that to you, but you know Maxi."

I did, and my grandmother would worry and that would spoil her day. "I'll try to come. That's the best I can do." Uncle Barney looked as if he wanted to speak but changed his mind.

He nodded. "Sometimes just trying to do something is the best any of us can manage."

I walked upstairs to my office to check my mail. There was nothing but junk mail, which I tossed into the wastepaper basket.

Leaving my Volvo in the agency parking lot, I walked the couple of blocks to the downtown business area. Maxi often reminisced about the local department store that used to be located across from the court-house. A couple of decades ago it was converted into rather pricy condos for the young and the hip—hip by Westport standards, anyway.

Wishing that the department store were still there to help me find Mother's Day presents for my mother and for Maxi, I strolled down the sidewalk and looked into the windows of the small shops.

My mother married several times after my father's death, always to men who were successful and well-to-do. Whenever I heard the phrase "a woman who has everything," I thought of her.

In Odds N' Ends, a crowded antique store where junk sat next to treasure, I found a small porcelain pill box with hand-painted violets on the lid. Perfect for my mother.

The best of the small shops, in my opinion, was the secondhand bookstore. As soon as I entered, I looked for Ferdinand, the resident cat. The big black-and-white male with the gorgeous green eyes was sprawled on the cookbook shelf. Judging by his girth, that was the appropriate section for him. I walked over and petted him. He rewarded me by purring like a percolator.

An hour later I'd selected three books for myself and an old illustrated volume of German poetry for Maxi. Looking at my purchases, I knew I'd made the decision to go to the cookout.

Before I returned to Victoria Grove, I phoned Joan Bower at the main bank and explained that I wanted to start interviewing the tellers. However, Friday was our busiest day. Should I wait until Monday, or could she send someone to take my place?

She consulted with her assistant and promised that a teller would be at the branch bank by one o'clock.

After a quick lunch of a bagel sandwich and a latte and the purchase of a pound of Costa Rican coffee at The Fragrant Grind, I drove back to the bank. Might as well get started on the interviews.

Mr. Bailey took the substitute teller and introduced her to Edward, who introduced her to the other tellers.

I instructed Elaine to send each of the tellers into my new office as they came upstairs.

I had made file folders for each teller. On a single sheet of lined paper, I listed the pertinent information from their employment records. In most cases that took up less than half a page. That's how little information the bank had on its employees. I couldn't decide whether that was due to reticence or negligence.

Louise Ballard came first. She was thirty-eight years old, divorced, with one dependent. A little on the plump side, with her dark blond hair frosted, she was an attractive woman. And visibly nervous.

"Is the bank laying off tellers?" she blurted out.

I was taken aback. "No. What did Mr. Bailey tell you?"

"Just that you wanted to speak with each of us."

Silently I called Clark Bailey a few choice words. He had undoubtedly scared the living daylights out of his employees with visions of layoffs. Part of that was my fault. I hadn't provided him with a script, but with many years' experience as a manager, I hadn't thought he would need one. Obviously I had been wrong.

"The bank isn't laying off anyone. How could they? I know from my experience as a teller how busy you are. And with a second subdivision going up just east of here, you'll be even busier." I smiled at her reassuringly.

"Management in Westport decided to use a different model of record-keeping in the human resources departments," I improvised, hoping that this didn't sound completely addle-brained.

I risked a quick look at Louise. She nodded, looking at me expectantly. Apparently my explanation didn't sound too far-fetched. Recalling the various school administrations I'd worked for during my counseling career, I knew the ways of the higher-ups were incomprehensible more often than not.

"I want you to fill out this form and then I'll ask you some questions. Some may be personal, but the purpose of the whole interview is to make employees more satisfied, because satisfied employees are more productive and efficient." I couldn't believe I had just trotted out this old chestnut. If I didn't stop with this twaddle, I'd make myself sick to my stomach.

I handed her the clipboard with a short, generic personality questionnaire and a number-two pencil.

It took Louise five minutes to bubble in her choices. I placed the form into her folder.

"You listed one dependent?"

"Yes. My daughter, Stephanie. She just turned fifteen."

Louise stopped and bit her lower lip.

"Fifteen. A difficult age," I said.

"Isn't that the truth," Louise murmured and drew a shuddering breath.

I didn't have to fake the sympathetic expression on my face, having dealt with what seemed like hordes of fifteen-year-old girls in school. Even the nicest of them were thinly disguised drama queens who could turn a serene saint into a raging hag in mere minutes.

"Stephanie was such a sweet child. Affectionate. Good-natured. I don't know what went wrong. What I did wrong."

"Is she in trouble?"

"All the time, anymore."

I could tell she was fighting tears. I couldn't count the number of times parents had broken down in my office at school, wondering what they had done wrong, blaming themselves, feeling like total failures. Though rarely was the trouble only one person's fault, more often than not, I silently assigned the greater guilt to the offspring. To my eternal shame, there had been moments when I'd wanted to slap the sullen, sneering, ungrateful, resentful, pimple-faced adolescents. To my credit, I had never succumbed to this urge.

"Tell me about the trouble," I said.

What Louise told me was the usual tale of teenage rebellion, drug experimentation, drinking parties, and total disrespect toward the parent.

"Have you tried counseling?"

Louise nodded. "Stephanie refused until she got expelled from school."

I pushed the box of tissues toward Louise. "She's in counseling now?"

"Yes. She's been at the Hamilton Center for the past month. The school said they wouldn't let her back in unless she got help."

"The people at the Hamilton Center are very good at what they do." I had worked with most of them and knew they were competent and committed to helping troubled kids.

"I wish I could afford to keep her there longer, but the place is so expensive and I don't have any money left. I'm broke. Wiped out."

Motive. Blast. I didn't want Louise to be the embezzler. It seemed to me that she had enough on her plate with a troublesome teenager.

"Have you asked for a loan from the bank?"

"I'm still paying off the last loan. I can't ask again." Her voice broke.

She was telling the truth about that. And probably about most everything else. "There are a couple of agencies that can help," I told her. "I'll bring you the forms to fill out. We might be able to extend Stephanie's stay at the Hamilton Center for a week or two. Wouldn't that help?"

"Every day she's in there and away from her nogood boyfriend is a blessing."

"You don't approve of him?"

"He's thirty-two years old! Would you want your teenager going out with a man more than twice her age?"

I shook my head emphatically.

"And it's not only the age. He's had more jobs in six months than I've had in my entire life."

"Stephanie's a minor. You can probably get a

restraining order against him. Possibly charge him with statutory rape."

"If I charged him with rape, Stephanie would run off and I'd never see her again. And a restraining order? He'd probably not come to the house, but he'd get her to meet him somewhere else. She thinks she's in love with him. Keeps hinting that when she turns sixteen I'll sign the permission form so she can get married. Over my dead body! The only thing that might get him to leave her alone would be if I gave him a bunch of money. But I don't have any."

More motive. How tempting would it be to a mother to take money from the dormant accounts to protect her child? Very tempting.

"What's his name?" I asked.

"Deacon Harris."

"You think he might have had problems involving the police?"

"It wouldn't surprise me," Louise said.

Me neither. A three-decades old guy who dated an underage girl would hardly be burdened with an over-whelming sense of ethics, even if his first name did evoke images of church elders.

"Does Deacon live in Westport?"

"Yes."

That was a break. I would consult Sam, my police detective cousin, to see if Deacon had a criminal record in Westport. To get information out of word-stingy

Sam, I'd have to invite him to a meal. Faced with a big plate of food, he became almost loquacious.

"I think that's all for now, Louise. I'll get those forms for Hamilton Center to you tomorrow."

She thanked me and left.

I made some notes and then asked Elaine to send in the next teller.

Agnes Miller came in, sat in the visitor's chair, crossed her legs, and folded her arms over her chest. Though her posture looked defensive, maybe even defiant, the jiggling of her foot betrayed her nervousness.

"What's this about?" she demanded.

I pretty much used the line I'd used with Louise but Agnes didn't buy it. Her disbelieving smirk plainly told me so. I decided to ignore her skepticism.

I asked her to fill out the same personality test I'd given Louise. When she'd finished, I said, "Heather told me that your mother passed away recently."

"Yes."

"I'm sorry."

Agnes shrugged. "She'd been sick for a long time, and after her stroke, I had to put her into a nursing home."

"How long did she stay there?"

"Almost three years."

"That ran into serious money."

"Tell me about it," she said, her tone dry. "We used up all our savings. I sold her car and mortgaged the house. If she'd hung on any longer, I don't know what I would have done."

Motive. In spades. The temptation to dip into the dormant accounts must have reared its seductive head. And Agnes was an experienced teller. She doubtlessly knew how to access those accounts without leaving a trail.

"I'm sure the bank would have given you a loan. After all, you've worked here for . . . how many years?"

"Twenty-one. The kind of loan I would have needed would have enslaved me to this place for the rest of my life."

There was more than a trace of resentment in her voice, which she tried to mitigate with a deprecating smile. I waited. My counseling experience had taught me that if I remained silent long enough, I could get anyone talking. Most people were uncomfortable with long silences.

"I suppose you think that because I'm not married and have no family, I should be satisfied to stay in this one-horse town."

Somebody had said that to her. I wondered who. Her mother? I remembered seeing a small framed photo next to her computer. "You have a pet?"

A warm look spread over her face. "Yeah. I have a dog. Hiram. He's a real sweetie."

"What would you like to do if you had your druthers?"

"Go down to the Indy 500 race. To Daytona. Buy a decent car. Travel. See something of this world. Hiram is a good little traveler. I'd take him along. He'd like that."

"Traveling sounds good to me, too." I had noticed her silver charm bracelet before but only now noticed that most of the charms had to do with cars. "I like your bracelet. Are those racing cars?"

"Yes."

She extended her arm across the desk so I could see the charms. "They are exquisite," I said. "Heather had beautiful bracelets, too."

"I wouldn't know," she said, her tone brusque.

"You weren't friends?"

"No. I hardly knew her. We didn't fraternize."

Interesting that she felt she had to stress not knowing the dead teller. The lady protested too much. And something Heather had told me, something having to do with Agnes, nagged at me.

After she left, I walked down the mezzanine to look at the display case that held trophies, pictures, and newspaper clippings of bank events. And there it was: a photo of Heather and Agnes after they'd won the bridge tournament sponsored by the bank.

Why had Agnes lied to me? Especially about something I could check so easily?

Chapter Four

Glancing at my watch, I saw that I had time for one more interview. Since Susan and I had worked in adjoining teller's cages, she had talked to me daily. I doubted that there was much about her home situation or financial status that I didn't already know. I asked Elaine to send for Carol Cornwell.

The bruise on Carol's face had faded to yellow. "Your face looks better," I said kindly.

She looked at me, alarmed.

Had she thought the makeup had hidden the bruise? "You know, you don't have to put up with abuse," I said gently. "There are people and agencies that can help you."

"I don't know what you're talking about," she said, looking at the floor. Her fair complexion had reddened.

"Carol, I used to be a social worker. I've seen enough wife beatings to recognize all the signs."

"Frank was drunk. He promised he'd never do it again."

Her expression was sheepish but also defiant, daring me to question her assertion. I suppressed a groan of disbelief. "Is he going to AA meetings?"

"Well, no. He says he doesn't need them. That he's no alcoholic."

Did she really believe this? I shook my head. "He'll get drunk again. And he'll slap you around again." I lifted my hand to stop her from interrupting. "How many times has he said he was sorry? How many times has he promised not to hit you again? Twice? Three times? A dozen? Too many times to count?"

"This time he means it," she said, her expression sullen.

Yeah, right, I felt like saying, but didn't. On a piece of paper I wrote the phone numbers of the women's help line and my cell phone. "Please take this and put it into your purse. At these numbers are people who can help you when you're ready."

She hesitated. Then she slipped the paper into her purse.

There was nothing I could do until she admitted that she needed help. Right now she was knee-deep in denial. I knew from experience that all my pleas, my recitations of statistics, my exhortations were useless at this point.

I handed her the personality test and delivered my spiel about the bank.

Since the downtown stores in Westport stayed open late on Friday nights, I decided to take Heather's bracelet to a few jewelers. Maybe someone remembered inscribing it.

I struck out in the three stores downtown. Just as I was ready to give up and go home, I remembered the jewelry store that was housed in a narrow building at the edge of the business district, where buildings turned into apartments and bed-and-breakfasts.

Although I had passed the store many times, I had never entered Himmelich & Son. As I did, I stopped just inside the door, unprepared for what I saw. It was all dark, gleaming wood, Persian rugs, and wrought iron light fixtures. A turn-of-the-century world.

"Can I help you?"

"I love your store!" I couldn't help exclaiming. "It's beautiful."

"Thank you. We get that reaction a lot. Or the question about when we'll come out of the Dark Ages."

"Oh, please don't remodel."

"We won't."

The man reassuring me was somewhere in his forties, so I assumed he was the grandson of the original Himmelich.

"I wonder if you can help me. I need to know if you remember this bracelet and the inscription."

He took Heather's bracelet and examined it under a

lamp. He nodded. "Yes. I inscribed it. I remember it because it's usually the giver of a piece of jewelry who has it inscribed, not the recipient."

I looked at him, waiting.

"The young woman, Heather, brought in the bracelet and asked me to inscribe it for her. I did. Is there some problem?"

"She's dead."

"I'm sorry. She was so young."

"Is there anything else you remember? The car she came in . . ."

He nodded. "As I said, her request was a bit unusual, so I walked to the window and watched her walk away."

Cynically, I wondered if he would have watched had Heather been old and homely.

"She got into a big car that was waiting for her down the block."

"What kind of car?"

"A Cadillac. Dark color. It had a Jesus fish on the back."

I crossed my fingers. "Did you notice the license plate?"

"Michigan plates, but that's all I remember."

"You've been very helpful. Thanks." I picked up the bracelet, flashed him a smile, and left.

On Saturday morning I reported to Uncle Barney. I had interviewed all the tellers except Edward.

"Why did you save him for last?" Uncle Barney asked.

I frowned. "Actually, I didn't. He chose to be last. He's the head teller. I think he enjoys this position a lot."

"What's he like? Is he married?"

"No." I had a hard time visualizing Edward as a husband. He struck me as an almost asexual being.

"What's he like?"

I closed my eyes to visualize him. Bow ties. Fancy suspenders. Small steps that would have made his walk mincing except for the slight limp. "He's an odd duck. A little prissy. Very fastidious. Sort of old-maidenish in his manner. He's good at his job. He loves gossip. I could be wrong, but I think there's a bit of a malicious streak in him."

"You're probably not wrong. You have a talent for pegging people."

"I'm not sure it's a talent. Maybe it's more of a case of listening and observing. Anyway, Edward's also the only one who has no motive for pilfering from the dormant accounts," I pointed out.

"At least none that we have found."

"Right. Has Glenn had any success in tracing the cuff link?" I asked.

"Not yet. Don't be discouraged. These things take time."

"True, unfortunately. I'll see you tomorrow at the picnic."

On my way home, I stopped at the hardware store for more paint. I had almost finished painting the wainscoting in the dining room of my Victorian fixer-upper when I ran out of paint. The bisque white really looked great with the colorful wallpaper, which reminded me of a William Morris design. My plan for the day was to finish the painting job and to prepare the potato salad I was taking to Maxi's celebration.

We all pitched in to help Maxi clean up after the picnic. Actually, *picnic* was too pedestrian a word for the sumptuous meal we'd just finished in the orchard. Maybe luncheon *al fresco* was a more accurate term.

"How are you holding up, *Schatzi*?" Maxi asked me.

"I'm not going to fall apart."

"Of course you're not," my mother said. Looking accusingly at Maxi, she added, "Cybil is tougher than that."

Not nearly as tough as you, I wanted to say.

"Elizabeth, the stiff upper lip thing is vastly overrated," Maxi told her daughter.

"We've always disagreed about that," my mother said, one perfectly arched eyebrow lifting. "You always think a good cry fixes everything when all it does is ruin your makeup."

I could feel the mother-daughter tension build across three generations. Oh, we were always civil to one another, but underneath, currents of edginess, failed expectations, and regrets flowed between Maxi and her daughter and between my mother and me.

I knew I was a disappointment to my mother. She

was a truly beautiful woman, even without makeup, even at age fifty-two, with blond hair, forget-me-not blue eyes, and flawless, fair skin. I knew for a fact that she hadn't had any cosmetic surgery, but I also knew she wouldn't hesitate to have the surgery when she deemed it necessary.

Her petite figure let her get away with wearing a white linen pantsuit. When I wore something in linen it wrinkled dreadfully, even if I'd ironed it only a half-hour earlier. On her, the linen didn't dare wrinkle.

With my brown hair and sprinkling of freckles across my nose, I looked a lot like Maxi had looked when she was my age. My mother could forgive me my average looks if I made more of an effort with my appearance. She was always telling me that I carried myself beautifully and that I had a good figure, though a little on the muscular side due to all that swimming. But I didn't dress stylishly enough to please her. Even though I thought my chinos and green cable sweater looked fine for a picnic, I knew my mother had looked at them critically and had silently sighed. It wouldn't surprise me if she'd wondered once again where she'd gone wrong with me.

Periodically she dragged me along on one of her shopping sprees, which invariably ended in a fancy spa where I'd be subjected to a makeover and a bagful of cosmetics. I did try to follow the beauty regimen for a while, but before the week was over I found the ritual too time-consuming and boring. There were so many things in life I hadn't done yet that sitting at a makeup table for twenty minutes each morning seemed a total waste.

When the food was put away, I said, "I have to talk to Luke."

"You two are talking?" my mother asked.

"Mom, we've always talked."

"I mean, *really* talking? Are you ready to give up this odd career and go back to him?"

"Why is whatever I do never good enough?"

"Are you equating working undercover in warehouses and banks and heaven knows what with being married to a doctor? Being a member of the Junior League? Doing appropriate volunteer work? Associating with the right people instead of criminals and other lowlifes?"

My mother's third husband had been a doctor, and if he hadn't succumbed to a heart attack, I suspect she would still be married to him. She had loved being a famous surgeon's wife.

"Luke's a great guy. And a terrific doctor," she said.

"Yes, he is," I agreed without hesitation.

"*Schatzi*, go on. Elizabeth will help me with the coffee and dessert," Maxi said.

My mother didn't look particularly pleased, but I was so happy to escape another why-don't-you-return-to-Luke discussion that I practically ran out the door.

Uncle Barney and Luke were deep in conversation but stopped when I approached them. Their expressions made me wonder if I'd been the topic of discussion.

"Am I interrupting?"

"Not at all. Luke and I were talking about the Cubs' chances for a pennant this year."

"If I were you, I wouldn't get my hopes up," I said.

"You want to talk to Luke privately?" Uncle Barney asked, sounding as if he hoped I would.

"No. This is work-related, so I'd like you to stay." I turned to Luke. "How can I find out who owns a boat if all I know is its name?"

"Is it a motorboat or a sailboat?"

I closed my eyes to visualize the photos I'd seen in Heather's locker. "A sailboat."

"Any idea how big a sailboat?" Luke asked.

I gave him a look.

"The name?"

"*The Wolverine.*"

"That's a lucky break. With a name like that, I'd say she has a Michigan registry."

"One of the photos I found in Heather's locker showed a stretch of beach. It sure looked a lot like the area just north of South Haven."

"Then that's where we'll start," Luke said.

"We?"

"Yes. It's safer to sail with someone than sail alone."

Even though that sounded reasonable, I wasn't quite sure Luke hadn't made this up. "Okay. What day did you have in mind?"

"Thursday I'm free. If that's not convenient, you'll have to wait till the following week."

"I'm sure Mr. Bailey will give you the day off," Uncle Barney said.

"Be ready at nine," Luke said. "This will take some time. And pack a lunch for two, please."

I opened my mouth to protest his ordering me around, but he was helping me and had flashed me one of his sweet grins, so I snapped my mouth shut. It wouldn't kill me to fix lunch.

"Anything else I should know or do?"

"Bring a windbreaker and a scarf or a cap. The wind can get pretty brisk on the lake."

When the phone rang, waking me up out of a deep sleep, I was momentarily disoriented. My bedside clock said it was three-thirty. My first thought was that something had happened to my grandmother. I picked up the receiver.

"Hello? Hello?" I waited. "Hello?" Nothing, except maybe the sound of breathing. This was creepy. Then anger overtook the momentary surge of fear.

"Listen, whoever you are. I'm tired of you waking me up in the middle of the night. The phone company promised to put a tracer on this line, and they'll catch you and nail your hide to the nearest telephone pole, so cut it out."

I was bluffing, but it was amazing how quickly he hung up. Or she. A woman could just as easily make a crank call as a man. Was it the person who'd dumped me into the lake? If so, then the caller was a man.

It took me a long time to fall asleep again, so when it was time to get up, I felt groggy and sleep-deprived. I moved slowly. The water in my shower wasn't very hot, so I figured I needed a new water heater. Everything in the old Victorian house I'd bought when I moved out of the home I'd shared with Luke and Ryan was falling apart. I sighed.

When I got out of the shower, I discovered I was out of coffee, not having been to the grocery store in a couple of weeks. My hair proved obstinate, and I singed my favorite white blouse with the iron. All in all, not a great start to the week.

At the bank, things improved a little. Elaine made a pot of coffee, and though it wasn't nearly as good as the brew Lynn fixed at the agency, it was coffee. I inhaled a cup and was ready for the day.

Edward strolled in with a jaunty air. He wore a bright red bow tie and red-and-black suspenders over his blindingly white shirt.

"What's this about?" he asked, implying he suspected this was a waste of his time.

"Something the main branch requested. It's a short survey designed to make our services better and our tellers happier." I watched him roll his eyes, something I'd never seen a grown man do in a business setting. "I'll have to ask you some questions—"

"You want to know what happened to my leg?"

I hadn't planned to ask him, but if he offered the information, I would certainly listen.

"I had polio as a child. My dream had been to join the Coast Guard the way my daddy had, but polio took care of that. Must run in the family, because my cousin Elmer had it too. He became a pharmacist."

"I'm sorry about the leg," I murmured. "Where are you from?"

"Michigan. The Upper Peninsula. Ever been there?"

"No. Agnes is from there, too. Did you know each other before you joined the bank?" I asked.

"No. It's a small world, as they say."

He had been making eye contact before, but now he looked at the floor. I suspected he was lying about something. Surely not about knowing Agnes before she came to Victoria Grove? That made no sense. At least to me it didn't.

I glanced at the form, wondering what to ask him next. "Tell me something about yourself."

"What do you want to know?"

He didn't wait for an answer but plunged right in, the way people do who like to talk about themselves.

"I live alone in a house on the west side of town. Small, but nice. Well, that's not quite true. About living alone, I mean. I have a bird. Her name is Kiki. She's smart. Knows all sorts of tricks. And she hears anybody approaching the house long before I do. She's better than an alarm system. My neighbor's house has been broken into twice, but not mine. Kiki's screeches make her sound like she'd just as soon tear you apart with her beak as look at you."

He sounded as proud as a parent. I could understand that, remembering how proud I'd been when Ryan sat up for the first time—

"You have a pet?"

"No."

"They're great companions. You should get one. The animal shelter always has pets waiting to be adopted."

"I'll consider it."

"Well, if there's nothing else, I should get back to work." He stood.

"In a few minutes." I carefully considered how to word my next questions. After throwing tact to the wind, I decided to come right out. He loved gossip. Maybe he'd just answer it. "What can you tell me about the tellers? Anything unusual about any of them?"

Edward sat back down and crossed his legs. He folded his hands and rested them on his knee. "Well, Louise is always dieting. She'll lose a few pounds and then that girl of hers gets into trouble and Louise'll start eating everything in sight. Carol's husband not only beats her, but gambles. One time he lost everything in a card game and they had to declare bankruptcy. They even spent a couple of nights in the homeless shelter."

"How awful." I'd speak to Carol again and remind her that she had choices.

"Then there's Susan. Her whining has driven her

husband to seek . . . how shall I put it? Seek comfort in the arms of another woman?"

Edward's enjoyment of the misfortune of others, as well as his unctuous tone, began to get on my nerves, but I had asked him. He continued.

"And Agnes? You'd think a woman of her age would know better."

"About what?"

"About having a boyfriend." He snickered.

I looked puzzled before I realized Edward had stopped speaking for effect. I waited for the other shoe to drop.

"The boyfriend's a good fifteen years younger than she is. Maybe more."

"Men date younger women all the time," I said.

"Yeah, but young studs dating forty-year-old women? Not unless there's something in it for them."

"Like what?"

"Like the woman spending all her money on his racing car."

Agnes had mentioned loving car races. Still, it was her business whom she dated. I loathed the smirk on Edward's face. "There's one more thing. A short questionnaire that I want you to fill in," I said.

The rest of the day passed uneventfully. I interviewed three women for the teller's position vacated by Heather.

Heather. Days had passed and I was no nearer to finding out who'd poisoned her.

Poison. Traditional belief claimed that poison was a woman's weapon. Who were the women in Heather's life? I made a list and ended up with only the female tellers at the bank. I had found no other women's names in Heather's address book. Lots of men's names. I shuddered when I contemplated having to track them all down.

Staring at the names, I wondered whom Heather had blackmailed. None of the tellers were well-off. All could access the dormant accounts. So could Heather. Why force someone else to do it? To avoid the risk of being caught? Though the bank probably wouldn't press charges to avoid going public, they would undoubtedly dismiss the teller and use the banking blacklist to make sure she wouldn't get another job in a financial institution.

Whoever had killed Heather was still stealing from the dormant accounts. Time to do something about that.

I walked out on the mezzanine and looked at the tellers' cages below. The Victoria Grove branch had kept its old-fashioned charm. I loved the fine marble of the floor and the pillars, the intricate wrought iron of the cages, the aged patina of the oak counters, and the elegance of the turn-of-the-century light fixtures. Thank heaven somebody had possessed the good sense not to modernize this beautiful building.

The silence suddenly struck me. Vaguely I remembered Elaine asking me if I needed anything before she went home. Glancing at my watch, I noticed that the bank had closed an hour ago. Except for the security guard, I was alone. I was about to return to my office when I thought I heard a sound. I leaned over the railing and strained to see if I could detect movement. Though the security lights were on, it was dusky.

A shadow moved in the deeper shadows. Someone was in the bank who shouldn't be there. It could be the embezzler. If I could catch her red-handed, it would save days of tedious work. I had no choice but to investigate.

I slipped out of my pumps and crept down the stairs. At the bottom I paused to listen. At first all I could hear was the pounding of my heart. Then I heard what I thought was the soft tapping of computer keys. The sound seemed to come from the tellers' cages. Between them and me stood the oak service desk the customers used. In a crouch I moved toward the desk and cowered under it until the beating of my heart slowed.

Silence. Had I imagined the sound of the computer keys? Or had the embezzler heard me, and, like me, was listening, waiting?

I squinted at my watch. In ten minutes the security guard would make his rounds through the main floor. The embezzler had to know that. She would have to make a move soon. Take the money she had stolen some time during the day and dash out the back door or through the locker room. I wish I knew which one she'd choose.

Just when I was beginning to think I might have imagined the whole thing, I heard the computer key sound again. To my right. Taking a deep breath, I crab-walked toward the gate. Thank heaven my knees didn't creak, but my stockings made a faint, whispering sound. I swung the gate open and scooted through. Cautiously I stood up.

Suddenly, something smashed into the middle of my body, knocking the air out of my lungs. I fell to my knees and then onto the floor. I was conscious of nothing but extreme pain.

"Mrs. Quindt?"

If only that voice would shut up and leave me alone.

"Mrs. Quindt, can you hear me?"

I knew if I didn't respond the voice would keep on talking and making me hurt all over. I opened my eyes.

"Thank heaven, you're alive," the bank guard said.

"What happened?" I asked, my voice whispery.

"You tell me. I came down the steps, heard the east door slam, and before I could investigate who'd left, I heard you moan. That's all I know."

"Go quickly and see if there's a car leaving the parking lot or someone running."

When he left, I sat up and immediately felt a wave of nausea hit me. I leaned back against the counter, closed my eyes, and willed myself not to throw up. I stayed absolutely still until the guard returned.

"Didn't see anybody. The only car in the lot is mine. Where's yours?"

"Parked down the street."

He looked at me. "Are you hurt bad?"

I started to shake my head and winced. Movement intensified the nausea. "No."

"I should probably call an ambulance and the sheriff."

"No. I don't need an ambulance and Mr. Bailey would have a fit if we called the sheriff without talking to him first. Please phone him."

While he did that, I closed my eyes again. I knew I should phone Uncle Barney, but he'd insist on calling Luke and we'd go through the whole when-are-you-going-to-quit-your-job business again.

"Mr. Bailey's on his way," the guard said.

"Good."

"Sure you're not hurt bad, Mrs. Quindt?"

"Just got the wind knocked out of me."

By the time Mr. Bailey arrived I felt a little less nauseated.

The guard told him what had happened and I reported what had led me to come downstairs.

"You didn't catch a glimpse of the person who hit you?"

"No."

"You sure you don't need an ambulance? A doctor at least?"

"I'm married to a doctor. If I need something I'll phone him." I tried to get up but failed. "Please help me up." The guard did.

On my way to the nearest computer, I stumbled over something and almost fell. "What on earth?"

Mr. Bailey picked up a green canvas bag from the floor. "I guess that's what you were hit with," he said. "With rolls of coins in there, this is pretty heavy and as effective as a cosh."

I dragged myself to each computer and touched it.

"What are you doing?" Clark asked.

"Trying to see if any of the computers are warm. That would be the one she used to withdraw funds."

"This one's warm," he said, indicating my old computer. "The one used by the sub from the main branch."

"So our thief is crafty enough to obtain everyone's password. Who keeps the passwords?"

"Elaine. But the tellers all have an individual code to log on."

"She has those too?"

Mr. Bailey nodded.

"Most people keep such information close by. Taped under a drawer or under a desk blotter."

"It's supposed to be kept in the vault."

"And who can get into the vault?"

"Usually just me. And the auditors when they come."

"But it's not impossible for someone else to get in?" I knew for a fact that Elaine, as well as Agnes and Edward, had been in the vault.

"It's possible," he agreed reluctantly. "It's also possible that whoever was in the bank was an outsider who somehow got in."

"No way," the guard said. "I was here, and I make my rounds. I don't sit around drinking coffee."

"If it were an outside thief, why didn't he grab that canvas bag full of money that he hit me with? That would make more sense than trying to access someone's computer. No, this was an inside job."

"You're probably right," Mr. Bailey said gloomily.

"You want me to call someone? The sheriff?" the guard asked.

"No. We'll handle this."

"Let's look at the tapes from the surveillance cameras," I suggested.

The guard retrieved them and took them into the break room. He fast-forwarded the tape until the camera showed movement. We watched the whole scene twice without being any wiser about the intruder's identity.

"It could be anybody, what with the baggy sweatpants, buttoned-up shirt, and ski-mask," I said, discouraged.

"Except Edward. The intruder didn't limp," Mr. Bailey said.

"No, he or she didn't," I agreed, and touched my mid-section, which hurt. Mr. Bailey saw me wince.

"You need a ride home?" he asked me.

"No, thanks. My car's outside."

"But can you drive it?"

"Yes." The nausea had diminished and I could drive the few miles. Once I was home I'd crawl into bed and stay there till morning.

Then I remembered I had invited Sam Keller, my cousin, for breakfast in exchange for information. I groaned but I couldn't cancel. Surely by morning I'd feel better.

Chapter Five

Sam arrived promptly at eight the next morning. When he took off his sports coat and draped it over the back of the kitchen chair, I saw that he had switched from wearing his gun in a shoulder holster to wearing it clipped to his belt.

Noticing my curious expression, he said, "The shoulder holster's too hot in the summer."

While I poured him a cup of coffee, I asked about his family.

"The baby's fine. Walking now and getting into things and driving my wife crazy."

"Tell Peggy again how much I appreciate her doing my taxes."

"You paid her, so no thanks are necessary. She's taken on a couple of clients. Small businesses. She does their books. Loves it. And is a whole lot easier to live with," he admitted, looking sheepish.

"Let me tell you something. Being a mother and a housewife is no picnic. No matter how much mothers love their babies, they need a little adult conversation, adult activities, to keep from going stir-crazy." I remembered I'd kept a few clients from my counseling job whom I saw in the evenings after Ryan was in bed.

"I'm sorry, Cybil. I shouldn't talk about the baby. It's gotta be hard for you—"

"Don't be silly. Of course I want to hear about Kaylee. Life goes on." I turned quickly toward the stove and removed the dish from the oven. I checked to see if the tortillas were warm. They were.

"We're ready to eat. *Huevos rancheros.*" Knowing Sam's hearty appetite, I placed two tortillas on his plate and topped them with the bean-tomato mixture and poached eggs. I'd also made some extra toast.

Sam dug in. After a couple of hefty bites, he paused to say, "This is so good. Cybil, if you get tired of your present job, please open a restaurant. I swear I'll be your most faithful customer."

He always said that. I smiled. I'd forgotten how satisfying it was to cook for a man who enjoyed food. Luke had always liked my cooking too. Maybe that's why I rarely cooked these days—there was no one in my house whom I could watch eat with gusto.

Sam polished off a second helping with more toast before he leaned back with a satisfied smile. He took a pack of filtered cigarettes from his shirt pocket and looked at me.

"Do you mind?"

I gave him a disapproving look but got up and fetched an ashtray. "You know these will kill you."

"If a bullet doesn't get me first."

As disquieting as the thought was, he was right. His job was dangerous. I started to clear the table.

"Leave the toast, please."

After refilling our coffee cups, I sat down and looked at Sam expectantly.

He removed one of those little notebooks he always carried and flipped the pages. "Okay. Here's the guy you asked me about at Maxi's party. Deacon Harris. Thirty-one. Has a juvenile record which is sealed, of course. Has been picked up a few times for being drunk and disorderly and for disturbing the peace but nothing heavy." He shut the notebook.

"Deacon doesn't have a job. How does he live?" I wondered out loud.

"A good question. I'll poke around a little. Talk to the guys on his beat." Sam looked at me searchingly. "And you're interested in this guy . . . why?"

"One of the tellers at the bank told me about him. She'd like to get him out of her daughter's life."

"Well, I realize Deacon is no altar boy, but I've seen worse."

"So have I. Imagine Kaylee being fifteen. Would you like her to date Deacon?"

Sam nearly choked on the piece of toast he was nibbling. I brought him a glass of water.

"We might be able to bring him in for contributing to the delinquency of a minor," he offered.

"No good. If you bring him in on any charge having to do with the girl, she'll blame the mother and that'll make everything worse."

Sam consulted his notebook again. "Seems he hangs out at that bar on the river, The Last Drop. Not exactly one of our finer watering holes. I'll have a word with the cops on the beat. They can keep an eye on him. Sooner or later Deacon's bound to screw up and we'll nail him. Fifteen-year-old girls." He shook his head sorrowfully.

I walked Sam to the door and thanked him again. Then I had to lie down. I didn't feel all that great. My middle hurt like the devil. When I'd looked at myself in the mirror, I'd seen the beginnings of a beautiful bruise.

Mr. Bailey called to ask how I felt. He suggested that I take the day off. I was happy to do so.

Later, I phoned the agency.

"Uncle Barney, did you send Glenn to the bank to test for fingerprints?"

"Yes. He only found the tellers' prints. As they spell each other for breaks and lunch, the prints he found were on the computers legitimately."

"So that's a dead end."

"Yes." He paused. "Did you notice anything at all before you were hit? A smell? Perfume perhaps? A familiar movement?"

"A movement like a limp? It wasn't Edward. I doubt very much that his leg would allow him to move as fast as this person did." I closed my eyes and put myself back at the scene of the attack. "My attacker was agile. She moved quietly and quickly."

"And she must have been about your height. Definitely not taller," Uncle Barney said.

"How do you figure that?"

"A bag filled with bills and coins is heavy. Pretend you're swinging it at someone."

I did.

"Did you swing it high to aim at someone's head or straight from the shoulder?"

"Straight from the shoulder. It was too heavy to swing up." Then I realized what he was getting at. "I see what you mean. A tall person, swinging it straight, would have hit me in the head."

"Yes."

"That means it could have been any of the tellers. Except maybe Louise. She's a little on the heavy side. I don't know how fast she can move."

"Let's not rule out anybody yet. Get some rest, Cybil. Are you sure you don't need a doctor?"

"Positive. If I had any internal injuries, I'd know by now. I'm just sore."

After promising Uncle Barney I'd rest, I hung up. I kept my promise by taking a nap, but by mid-afternoon I was restless.

Not knowing what to do, I took a notebook and listed everything I knew about the tellers. Each woman needed money badly. Each had opportunities to access the dormant accounts. That established motive and opportunity—just as in Agatha Christie's mysteries. But no one had a reason to poison Heather. At least none that I had found. And each of them had lied to me about something, except Louise.

What about Edward? His financial situation was better than the women's. He'd had issues with Heather but they were in the past. According to him. Could he have secretly hoped that she would become his protégée again? People often harbored expectations that appeared purely delusional to others. Could he have felt betrayed enough to poison her? I thought about that question long and hard and came to no conclusion.

And who had dumped me into the lake? I'm not a large woman, but it still would have taken someone fairly strong to carry me to the car and then to the boat. And since I'd been unconscious, I had been dead weight. That raised another question: who had access to ether? How difficult was it to get? Luke might know. I would ask him.

Thursday morning dawned bright and sunshiny—a perfect day for sailing, according to Luke, who picked me up. On the drive to the lake, we talked with the ease that familiarity brings.

The *Sea Urchin*, which Luke had bought after our separation, looked small and fragile on the immenseness of Lake Michigan. Luke assured me that she was safe and that he was a good sailor. Remembering that he had sailed his parents' boat as a teenager, I managed to relax a little. I relaxed even more when he handed me one of those bright orange vests and put one on as well.

The sailboat was small enough that Luke could handle her alone. All I had to do was sit back and enjoy the ride.

"Cybil, put this on your face."

He tossed a tube of sunscreen at me. I caught it and smoothed the cream over my skin. "If I get more freckles, I'll get a lecture from my mother."

"I always thought your freckles were—"

"Luke, if you say *cute*, I'll push you overboard."

He grinned. "I was going to say sexy."

I flicked him a disbelieving look.

"Now I'm wondering, what's wrong with *cute*?"

"Nothing, when you're twelve. A mature woman prefers other terms. *Sexy* is a good word."

"I *was* going to say that."

"Here." I tossed the tube back at him. "Put some on your face. I remember the graphic lecture about melanoma you gave me."

I leaned back against the railing and closed my eyes.

The warmth of the sun and the gentle motion of the boat lulled me to sleep.

Some time later, Luke shook my shoulder. "Cybil, wake up. We're approaching the first marina."

After we docked, we walked into the marina's office. While Luke paused to inspect a stack of boat cushions, I approached the man behind the counter.

"We're looking for friends of ours. I know they keep their boat up here, but we forgot the name of the marina. Their last name's Jackson." I figured S.R. would keep the same identity he'd used at the motel.

"Doesn't ring a bell. I'm more likely to remember the boat's name."

"*The Wolverine.*"

He shook his head. "There are two more marinas in the area. And a yacht club. You might try them."

"Thanks." I joined Luke by the stack of cushions.

"You like any of these cushions?" he asked. "I could use some new ones for the boat."

"Those maybe," I said, pointing.

"Pink?"

"Don't sound so disapproving. You asked me. And they're not pink."

"You could have fooled me. If not pink, what?"

"Salmon. The color's got too much orange in it to be pink."

Luke shook his head. "I'm not having pink or salmon cushions on the *Sea Urchin.*"

"Picky or what? But suit yourself. Are we walking to the next marina?"

"And to the next if necessary. We'll find S.R."

We didn't. Discouraged, we returned to Luke's boat.

"Let's have lunch," he suggested. "I always think better on a full stomach. You know, fuel for the body and the brain. What did you bring?" he asked, his voice eager.

"We'll start with gazpacho. That's a salad in cold soup form. Very refreshing on a warm day." I divided the contents of the thermos between two plastic tumblers. "To better luck this afternoon," I said, raising my tumbler in a toast. Luke did the same.

"This is good," he said.

He also liked the chicken salad with green grapes and walnuts as well as the strawberries we dipped into a plastic bag filled with powdered sugar.

After we ate, Luke lay back and promptly fell asleep. So did I.

When I woke up some twenty minutes later, I studied him, wondering if he got enough rest, if he ate properly, went to the gym to work out. When we lived together, I'd seen to it that he did these things. Now it was up to him. He was a grown man, a physician, who knew how important these things were.

He looked good in cut-off jeans and a T-shirt. His body was as lean as when I first met him. Only the silver in his dark hair hinted at the years that had passed and the heartbreak of his son's death.

"Like what you see?" he asked lazily.

"I always have, but I'm wondering if you work too hard."

"Sometimes. Some days the ER is crazy and everybody stays whether it's quitting time or not. You know it's always been like that."

I remembered. I used to fall asleep on the couch, waiting for him to come home.

"Except now nobody waits for me. I don't like coming home to a silent, empty place."

I didn't particularly like it either, but I wasn't ready to give up my present life. I needed the isolation to wrap around me like a protective layer, like insulation. I sensed it helped me heal.

"What do we do now? Go home?" I asked.

"No. Remember the yacht club the first marina owner mentioned?"

I nodded. *The Wolverine* could be berthed there.

Luke got us under way and a half hour later we reached the yacht club.

We walked up to a man working on an outboard motor. He wore a ratty straw hat with fishing lures stuck in it, which made him look a little like the head honcho in the first episodes of "M.A.S.H." Henry something?

"Hi. We're looking for *The Wolverine*," Luke said.

"You just missed her. A bunch of members took her out for a trip up to Petoskey."

"Darn. When will they be back?" I asked.

"Saturday. But she's booked for another member and his party until Monday."

"The reason we're asking is that a member told us about the club," Luke said. "I wrote down the name of the club but only the guy's initials. S.R. I was sure I'd remember——"

I made that little disbelieving sound wives make. "You guys were killing a twelve-pack. What were the chances you'd remember?"

Luke looked at his feet and all but shuffled them.

"I saw the guy," I said. "If I describe him, maybe you'll remember him. Mid-fifties, in good shape, well-to-do, and from the Detroit area."

"That fits a lot of our members," the man said.

"When I saw him he was wearing a toupee. An expensive one. And he was with a pretty woman. Blond. Young." I saw him nod. He obviously remembered Heather.

"That rings a bell. My memory with names ain't that good anymore, but you can look at the list of members. Maybe you can spot this guy's name."

"Thanks," Luke said. On the way into the building, I met Luke's gaze. He shrugged. I thought he was thinking the same thing—the man was probably violating the privacy of the club members, but we weren't going to mention that to him.

We looked at the list, which gave names and home towns but no street addresses or phone numbers. I think we spotted the name simultaneously. *Sanford Rogers,* from Detroit. To make sure there was no other S.R., we looked at the entire list.

We thanked the man and returned to the *Sea Urchin*.

"Why does the name seem so familiar?" I wondered aloud.

Luke nodded. "Sanford Rogers. I know I've heard that name too, but I can't remember where."

"Uncle Barney will have someone at the agency find out who he is. I don't want to do a computer search at the bank."

"What happened to your laptop?"

"It died on me and I haven't had a chance to buy a new one." Actually, I had had to have a new roof put on my house, which had pretty much wiped out my savings account. I wasn't about to tell Luke that; he had told me that for someone who knew nothing about house repairs and upkeep to buy an old house was sheer lunacy. He was probably right, but the house had called out to me.

We sailed to the marina where Luke kept his boat and then drove back to Westport.

I'd spent a lovely day with Luke, which was followed by a plunge into depression. This happened often after I'd had time alone with Luke. I realized all over again just how much I had lost: my little boy and my happy marriage—everything that had started out happy and good and promising. It didn't help that the separation after our son's death had been mainly my idea.

I showered, crawled into bed, and cried myself to sleep.

Because I'd given in to my grief, I was determined the next day to stay super busy and get a lot done. I phoned Uncle Barney at the agency and gave him a verbal report. He too found the name of Heather's boyfriend familiar but couldn't place it.

At the bank I interviewed three more candidates for Heather's position. The rest of the time I spent on the mezzanine behind a pillar, watching what was happening on the floor below.

It struck me that the cameras were focused on the customers, not on the tellers. What if we had hidden cameras focused on the tellers? Could I spot the embezzler that way? Excited by the possibility, I phoned Uncle Barney.

He was quiet for long moments, making me fear I'd just proposed something totally asinine.

"That's not a bad idea, but is there a place to hide the cameras? And you'd need one for each teller. That also means that someone has to watch each tape, all eight hours of it. I suppose parts could be fast forwarded, but in order to catch the embezzler in the act, you'd pretty much have to watch all the tapes."

"Darn. Not such a great idea," I muttered, feeling disappointed.

"On the other hand, you'd only have to watch the

tapes for the day when one of the flagged dormant accounts was accessed and an illegal withdrawal was made. That would cut down the time considerably."

"You're right." I immediately felt better. "Uncle Barney, how have you hidden cameras in the past? I mean, what do you put the camera in?"

"All sorts of things. Cameras have gotten lots smaller, so it's easier now to hide them."

As he told me some of his more interesting hiding places, I kept visualizing the bank. Tellers had to take their own banking transactions to one of the other tellers. No one was supposed to do her own. So if I could spot one of them pocketing cash, I'd have the embezzler. Except nothing was that simple. I sighed. Absentmindedly, I wiped dust from the leaves of the plant on my desk. Then it hit me.

"I've got it. Hanging plants. On the wall behind the customers and facing the tellers. There are high windows on that wall. It would be a perfect spot for some of those plants in big baskets. And couldn't the cameras be hidden in the baskets?"

"Yes. We once used plants for just such camera surveillance. Worked well."

"How expensive is this going to be?" I asked.

"It won't be inexpensive, but given the fact that the bank is losing thousands to the embezzler, it's money well spent."

"Let's say Mr. Bailey goes for the idea. Who could do this for us?"

"I've just the man for the job."

While Uncle Barney told me about the particulars, I took notes.

Five minutes later I was in Mr. Bailey's office. I closed the door, earning me a surprised look. I told him about the project.

"The guy my uncle recommends is reliable and discreet. The agency has used his services in the past." When I gave him the rough quote, he winced.

"Ouch. I'm going to have to check with Joan Bower."

"In the long run, it'll save you thousands," I pointed out.

"Who's the guy who will install the cameras?"

"His name is Fox. Uncle Barney vouches for him. And he does good, fast work."

I left him to make his call.

Ten minutes later he told me to go ahead and make the arrangements.

I phoned Uncle Barney, who got in touch with Fox.

Later that afternoon my uncle called me and said that Mr. Bailey and I would have to go to the bank at five on Sunday so Fox could show us how the cameras worked, how to change the tapes, how to take care of the plants so that nobody else did and stumbled inadvertently on the surveillance.

Mr. Bailey wasn't happy that the cameras couldn't be installed immediately, and neither was I. The embezzler could withdraw big amounts every day and there was nothing I could do about it, no matter how much time I devoted to speculating about the thief's identity. Blast.

While waiting for the installation, I spent a lot of time each day in the break room. Mostly I listened to the women talk, while pretending to check columns of figures on computer printouts, which I then filed in three-ring binders.

The break room was divided into three areas. In the middle was a lounge/eating area with a television, to the right was a tiny kitchen, and to the left a ladies' bathroom.

When I entered the room on Thursday, the television was turned on low, as it always was, to the all-news station. I was probably better informed now about current events than at any time before. The room seemed empty, but then I heard water running in the bathroom. I was about to turn up the volume on the television when I heard a voice. It took a second before I realized a woman was talking on the phone. *Agnes*, I thought. I hadn't planned to eavesdrop, but something in her voice compelled me to listen.

Her voice rose in protest, then lowered in an attempt to persuade, then rose in trembling supplication. There was no doubt in my mind that she was speaking to a man, a man who meant something to her. The years-younger boyfriend Edward had mentioned?

Her voice rose in volume; I could hear every word she said. "Rafe Carson, you listen to me. I'm coming to the race on Friday. I paid for the lousy car. I have a right to see it in action."

Silence as she apparently listened to Rafe.

"I'll be at the racetrack. Don't you dare make a fuss and don't hang up on me," Agnes said. "Don't—"

The next thing I heard sounded like a trash can being kicked across the floor. Rafe had apparently hung up. I heard water running into the basin. I suspected that the noise was meant to drown out the sound of weeping. It didn't.

I turned my attention to the papers in front of me. Minutes later Agnes stormed out of the bathroom and out of the break room. I doubt she even noticed me sitting in the back.

A racetrack in Westport? How could I not have known that there was one? I phoned Glenn at the agency.

"Yeah, we got a racetrack," he confirmed. It's west of the airport on County Road 500."

"I've driven on that road countless times and never noticed a racetrack."

Glenn laughed. "You're probably thinking in terms of the Indy 500. This is a tiny miniature of that track."

I thought a *tiny miniature* was redundant but let it pass. "When do they have races there?"

"Friday nights, starting at six-thirty. Why this sudden interest in racing?"

"Might be part of this case."

"The embezzling? You're kidding."

"No. I know this sounds farfetched, but . . ." I had a glimmer of an idea. "Glenn, is racing an expensive sport?"

"Yes. Most racers have sponsors. Several, unless they get one of the big tire companies or motor oil companies to sponsor them."

"You've been to the Westport track?"

"Sure, but not recently. Who're you interested in?"

"Rafe Carson."

"Don't know the name, but I can ask around."

"Thanks. Call me as soon as you know something." I hung up and leaned back in my chair.

Agnes was Rafe Carson's sponsor. Not on her bank teller's salary, of course. She had a powerful motive for embezzling. But not for poisoning Heather.

Maybe I was wrong. Maybe the murder and the embezzling weren't related. Maybe Heather wasn't murdered. Maybe she had committed suicide. No. I might be wrong about everything else, but not about that. The death of my little boy had torn me apart and driven me to the very edge, but I hadn't killed myself. And neither had Heather. But who had killed her?

I reviewed everything I knew about her and about the other tellers. All this did was give me a pounding headache.

After work I drove straight to the YWCA, where I swam laps for thirty minutes. That and three ibuprofen cleared my headache.

The next day I headed to Maxi's farm for supper, comfort, and conversation.

Seated at her kitchen table, I watched her scoop up dough with a soup spoon and drop it into salted boiling water.

"My dumplings are never the same size. Yours are," I observed.

"Years of practice," she said with a smile. "In time yours will be too."

After she'd added the cooked dumplings to the chicken, red and fragrant from the sweet paprika, Maxi brought the food to the table. She served it with Bibb lettuce dressed with a simple vinaigrette.

The dinner, of which I ate too much, was delicious. I told Maxi so. While we did the dishes, she asked me how the case was going and if my sailing trip with Luke had been helpful.

"Yes. We found out who S.R. is. At least his name, which sounded familiar to both of us. You know how something can tease your mind and you've almost remembered, but then it slips away?"

"It will come to you."

"I need to call Uncle Barney and see if he's done a computer search on Sanford Rogers."

Maxi stopped in the middle of washing a place. "Sanford Rogers?"

"Yes. You know him?"

"Not personally. But on Sundays when I don't make it into town for church, I watch him on television. He's quite a charismatic preacher."

"Of course! The televangelist. Not as famous as some of them, but he seems to have a local following, doesn't he?"

"Oh, yes."

"And he is married?"

"His wife and children sing in the choir."

"So a scandal would hurt his career."

"What sort of scandal?" Maxi wanted to know.

"Adultery."

"That would definitely hurt him. He is big on family values, and adultery isn't one of them," Maxi said, her tone dry.

"Would it hurt his career enough that he might murder his paramour if she threatened to expose him?"

"Oh, my! I can't believe that a preacher would be capable of such a deed. And you can't believe it either. You're not that cynical."

I sighed. "I hate to think he poisoned Heather, but somebody did. I have to talk to him. I wonder where he lives."

"He'll be at a big tent revival this Sunday, about twenty miles north of here. We'll have to leave early to get seats."

"We?"

"Of course. You have never been to a revival, have you?" Maxi asked.

"No. Have you?"

"No, but I've watched them on television," she said with a grin.

"Won't there be a lot of people there?"

"Hundreds, at least."

"So how can we get near enough to speak to him?"

"Good question." Maxi thought for a minute. "Drive up early and canvass the area. You'll think of something."

I had to smile at Maxi's use of the word *canvass*.

She caught my smile. "Isn't that what you do, canvass?"

"Yes. We could use some help. Maybe Uncle Barney will let us have Glenn."

"Or he could come himself."

"He doesn't give up his Sunday golf game easily," I warned.

"I know, but it wouldn't hurt him to go to church, even if it's in a tent."

I was tempted to ask how much she was willing to bet on Uncle Barney's showing up, but decided not to. She was his mother, and once a mother, always a mother.

We finished the dishes.

"I have some plants for you," Maxi said. "You didn't buy any, did you?"

"No." I followed her to the small greenhouse Uncle Barney had built for her, using the windows she had replaced in the farm house.

"These are petunias. The deep purple ones you like because they have a light, pleasant smell. And these are white ones. They look good planted together."

"They'll go into the hanging baskets I bought for the back porch."

"And here are flats of zinnias, snapdragons, and tall marigolds. They'll look good in the bed bordering your front porch."

"Great. Thanks, Oma. I just hope I don't kill them."

"You won't. These are tough varieties that have stood the test of time. Just remember to dig the holes deep enough and don't forget to water them. We prepared that bed last fall by adding peat moss and black soil. You'll do just fine, *Schatzi*."

That was one of the best things about my grandmother. She always had great faith in me.

Chapter Six

At 5:30 on Friday I parked my car in the grassy parking lot of the Westport Race Track. Glenn was there too, planning to get information from an acquaintance whose son was one of the drivers.

I was amazed at the people I saw there. Ashamed, I realized that I had assumed that the audience would be a redneck crowd. Instead, at least half of them were families with children.

Walking around, I looked for Agnes. I knew she was there because I had spotted her car. I finally saw her near the door marked *Drivers Only*. She had shed the uptight teller's persona of the bank. Her hair curling softly around her face, wearing form-fitting jeans and high-heeled boots, she had morphed into an attractive woman. She kept looking at her watch, obviously waiting for someone. I sat down several rows away, determined to see who it was.

Ten minutes later a twenty-something guy carrying a duffle bag approached the door. He exchanged a few words with Agnes. When he made a move toward the door, Agnes laid her hand on his arm to stop him. He listened to her, his expression sullen, bored. He looked around to see if anyone was paying attention to him. When a couple of giggling teenaged girls caught his attention and asked him for his autograph, he shook off Agnes's hand and signed the girls' programs with a flirtatious grin. Then, preening, he walked through the drivers' door without a glance at Agnes, who looked as if she'd been kicked in the stomach.

I felt compassion for her and anger toward the young stud. From the way she had looked at him, it was obvious that she was in love with him. It was equally obvious that he did not feel the same way. I pegged him as being capable of that casual, careless male cruelty that could break a woman's heart without half trying.

Glenn joined me. "That young Turk was Rafe Carson," he said, obviously having witnessed the scene also.

"I was afraid of that. Is he any good as a race driver?"

"Not nearly as good as he thinks he is. I admit he looks the part, but he's too cautious to make it big. He had a sponsor but lost him."

I waited, suspecting that there was more to the story.

"Seems Rafe had a thing going with the sponsor's wife."

"Not very smart of him," I said.

"No, he's not the sharpest knife in the drawer. But women don't seem to care about that. They throw themselves at him. Must be nice."

"You sound a little wistful. Wouldn't it get boring? Women throwing themselves at you?"

"I wouldn't know. None of them have thrown themselves at me." Glenn heaved an exaggerated sigh.

"Since he lost his sponsor, who's financing his racing?"

"That's the question of the hour. My friend speculates that it's a woman who hangs out at the track. Older than him."

"A woman who should know better," I muttered. Agnes had just moved to the top of my list of embezzlers. "Anything else?"

"You're not going to like this," Glenn warned.

"I already don't like any of this. What?"

"He's got a girlfriend on the side. A young one."

"What? That scum. That miserable little twerp. I'd like to rip his . . . ears off."

Glenn grinned. "I knew you wouldn't like it."

Agnes, if she was the embezzler, was risking serious prison time for this ingrate, and what did he do? Cheat on her. Men could be such jerks.

The races started, but I didn't pay much attention.

Speed had never fascinated me. Frankly, grown men driving little cars around an oval at frightening speeds seemed fairly pointless to me. I stayed until Rafe did his thing. He didn't do it very well. But he did look good in his silver outfit. Judging by the expression on Agnes's face, she thought so too.

When she saw me approach, she looked as if she wanted to bolt, but it was too late. I greeted her with a smile.

"I didn't know you were a race fan," she said.

"I'm not, but my friend is," I said, nodding toward Glenn, who was buying us a couple of soft drinks.

"You did all right out there," I said to Rafe, who smiled, pleased. Agnes introduced us, but before we could get acquainted, Rafe was called away.

"He seems nice," I said, hoping I sounded convincing. Apparently I did, for Agnes fairly beamed at me.

"He is, but not everyone sees that in him. Some people can't get past his good looks."

Guiltily I admitted to myself that I hadn't. Perhaps he was nicer—no, not when he had a girlfriend on the side.

"Well, I better rejoin my friend," I said and left.

On Saturday I planted the flowers Maxi had given me. By the time I was done, I felt done in. And here I'd thought I was in good shape. Of course, none of the exercises I did included squatting close to the ground and digging holes.

Maxi came to spend the night with me so we could

leave bright and early the next morning for the revival meeting in southwestern Michigan. As I'd expected, Uncle Barney pleaded a prior commitment on another case and couldn't go with us.

"You did a good job planting," Maxi said, inspecting my gardening efforts. "Remember to feed the plants once a month and pick off the dead blooms on the petunias. And water them but don't drown them."

I decided that every Friday after work would be my gardening time. And maybe Sunday afternoon if the weeds threatened to take over.

We had just entered the kitchen when someone knocked on the back door.

"I'll get it," Maxi offered, looking a little guilty.

Suspecting who the caller was, I shook my head at Maxi. My grandmother was hopelessly optimistic.

"Hi, Luke," she said and returned his hug.

Luke looked at me, waiting for me to invite him in. "Come on in," I said, resigned.

"*Schatzi*, I picked the first spinach of the season and I know how much both of you like it, so I invited Luke to join us. I hope you're not angry with me."

"I'm not."

Luke grinned delightedly. "You're fixing your creamed spinach with the poached eggs . . . what do you call it?"

"*Spinat mit Spiegeleier.*"

Luke rubbed his hands with a happy smile. "What can I do?" he asked, rolling up his shirtsleeves.

I took the loaf of golden bread from Maxi's basket and handed it to him. "You can slice the bread. I'll wash the spinach." I filled the sink with cold water and dumped the dark green leaves into it. The grit and sand clinging to the spinach sank to the bottom of the sink. Then I scooped the leaves into a colander and repeated the process twice more with fresh water.

Twenty minutes later we ate at the kitchen table. For a meal as simple as this, it was utterly satisfying and delicious.

After dinner I walked Luke out.

"You will be careful tomorrow," he said.

Maxi had told him of our plan to try to see the tele-vangelist. "Just how dangerous do you think going to a revival meeting is?" I demanded.

"It shouldn't be dangerous at all, but it's a profitable business and nobody likes their profits endangered." He placed his hands on my shoulders and urged me closer.

In the dim light of the evening I couldn't read his expression, but I thought he might look a little worried.

"I don't like your taking Maxi with you—"

"*I'm* taking Maxi? She invited herself and couldn't be talked out of it. You know how stubborn she can be."

"She's also seventy-five years old."

That hit me wrong. I stepped back, forcing him to release my shoulders. "I know how old my grandmother is. She would be insulted if she knew you thought she was too old to go to a revival meeting. You want to tell her she is?"

"No," Luke admitted, tugging on his earlobe. "It's just that if anyone can get into trouble at a revival meeting, it's you, Cybil."

"There will be no trouble," I maintained staunchly. "Good night, Luke."

Later, as I lay in bed, I didn't feel quite as confident. Sanford Rogers could have poisoned his lover. If Heather threatened him, threatened to tell his wife, he might have been driven to a rash act. He had a lot to lose. And my asking questions wasn't going to make him happy.

We left early, just in case we got lost. We didn't. The way to Baxter's Meadow, the site of the revival, was clearly marked. The tent was already up and a crew was busy setting up folding chairs.

"Can you believe the size of the crowd they seem to be expecting?" I asked.

Maxi shook her had. "And look at the vendors."

A hot dog stand was going up next to a wagon selling ice cream, which was flanked by a booth selling sandwiches and salads.

"This looks more like a fair than a religious ceremony," I muttered.

"Well, people get hungry."

Being used to a twenty-minute sermon and some hymns and prayers, all of which lasted about an hour at the Sunday morning service at my church, I was truly dumbfounded by the spectacle unfolding around us.

"How long does this revival last?" I asked.

"Probably till evening."

I simply stared at Maxi.

"There will be several preachers."

"Hey, sister, over here."

I looked around to see the person addressed as *sister*, but there was no one there.

"You're here early to help, ain't you?"

"Yes, we are," Maxi said cheerily.

I grabbed her arm to hold her back but she wouldn't be stopped.

"What is it you want us to do?" she asked with an eager smile.

"Hand out these bulletins to folks as they come in."

"We can do that," Maxi said. "By which door does the preacher come in?"

The man frowned at Maxi, but seeing her benign smile, he said, "Back there." He pointed to the entrance near the microphones.

"Then we'll take this door," I said, fixing him with a long look that dared him to disagree.

"Fine by me." He handed each of us a stack of bulletins and rushed off.

"What's your plan?" Maxi asked in a low voice.

"I assume that at some point Sanford Rogers will take a break. He'll come out that entrance. With us stationed here, I might have a chance to speak to him." It wasn't much of a plan, but I couldn't think of anything else.

For the next hour or so we were kept busy handing out bulletins. To my amazement not only was every folding chair taken, but people also stood three deep inside the perimeter of the tent in a semicircle facing the microphones.

The choir arrived. There had to be thirty singers, all wearing burgundy robes. They were good, spirited, and loud, all but shaking the tent. As Maxi had said, Sanford Rogers was impressive. I noticed that he wasn't wearing his toupee. Had he worn it with Heather as a disguise, or in an effort to appear younger?

As expected, the sermon contained some fire-and-brimstone exhortations but there was more to the homily than that. He was a forceful speaker, frequently interrupted by the crowd's shouts of *hallelujah!* and *amen*.

"What do you think of the service?" Maxi whispered.

"A little too emotional for me."

When the choir launched into another number, I backed out of the tent and hurried toward the preachers' entrance. For once I was in luck. Sanford Rogers came out, wiping his brow with a large white handkerchief. He was followed by a couple of preachers and several men who looked like bodyguards. How could I get close enough to speak to him? Before I could think of a way, he went back inside.

Drat. I fumed for a few minutes, fanning myself with the stack of bulletins I still had in my hand. A note. If I could persuade or bribe the young man guarding the preachers' tent to hand the note to Preacher Sanford, perhaps he'd speak with me. I considered and discarded several versions before I settled on a straightforward approach.

I need to speak with you about Heather Atkins.
This is not a shakedown.
Cybil Quindt.

I wrapped the note in a twenty-dollar bill and handed it to the man guarding the entrance.

"Could you please give this note to the preacher when he comes out again? It's really important."

The young man smirked a little, as if I were asking for a clandestine meeting. Were televangelists pursued by groupies?

"Okay, sister," he said, whisking the money into his pocket.

This was a gamble, of course. I might have just wasted twenty dollars. Still, this *was* a religious gathering, and truth and honesty might triumph over greed and mendacity.

Forty-five minutes later, Sanford Rogers came out of the tent again. I watched the guard point at me as he handed over the note. The preacher read it and started to walk toward me. I met him halfway.

"Let's walk," he said. "What makes you think I knew this Heather?"

Was he going to lie and deny knowing Heather? Or

was he just being cautious? "I worked next to her at the bank." I could almost see him struggle between facing up to knowing Heather and denying it. In the end truth won. I was glad.

"Did Heather confide in you about us?"

"No. She was discreet. I found out because the bank sent me to her apartment to do an inventory. I found a cuff link that essentially led me to you."

"What do you want from me?"

"Where were you the night of her death?"

He stopped walking and looked at me. "What are you getting at? The newspaper article said she committed suicide."

"I don't believe that. Do you?"

"No. It's out of character. I think she accidentally took an overdose."

"Heather had no trouble sleeping. Why would she take a pill? Especially one so large she couldn't have swallowed it. I think somebody slipped the sleeping pills into her drink."

"And you suspect me?"

A hard edge had crept into his voice as he leaned toward me. I almost stepped back but stopped myself. "Did you?"

"No." He wiped his brow again. "I broke several Commandments, but not the Sixth." He looked at the ground. "Why would I poison her?"

"Maybe you felt threatened. You do have a wife and a career that would be damaged by a scandal, if not destroyed. Maybe Heather got tired of being the other woman. Maybe she tried blackmailing you."

"She didn't blackmail me. And my wife is aware of my . . . weakness."

"Does . . . did your wife know about Heather?"

"No. At least I don't think so."

"What would she have done if she had known?"

"Hard to say. She forgave me once or twice in the past."

"But she might not have done so this time. A woman's patience isn't inexhaustible. A scandal involving another woman would be embarrassing to her and your children. Not to mention damage your career, or even destroy it."

"I wouldn't kill to save my marriage or my career. I'm no saint, but I wouldn't fall that low." He sighed. "I tried not seeing Heather for a while, but I couldn't stay away for long. In time I would have. Or Heather would have ended it. She knew from the start that there was no future for us. She was a free spirit who lived only for the moment. That was incredibly exciting to a man like me, whose every minute is planned."

"Are you connected with a Bible college?"

"Yes. Why do you ask?"

"I found a brochure in Heather's desk." I waited. Finally I said, "You haven't told me where you were the night she died."

"I was at a revival meeting on the Upper Peninsula. Several hundred people saw me there. The meeting went on till midnight. There's no way I could have gotten back to Westport in time to poison Heather. You can check. The television station up there filmed part of the revival."

He took a business card from his pocket and wrote the station's name on it. "You can check by calling them."

I accepted the card and dropped it into my handbag.

"Were you in Heather's apartment when I came to do the inventory?"

"Yes. I'm sorry I pushed you down. I panicked when you came in."

"You were looking for . . . ?"

"The cuff link. My wife had them made for me."

"I'll mail it to you if it turns out you're innocent."

"Thank you. I am innocent. At least of murder. I loved Heather in my fashion. Believe that or not. You do what you have to do."

"I will. And no one will find out about your relationship unless you're somehow involved in her death."

"Fair enough. I hope you find out who killed her. Be careful."

One of the men called to him to go back inside. He turned and walked toward the tent, his shoulders drooping a little as if he were suddenly exhausted.

Maxi was waiting for me. "Are you ready to go home?" she asked.

"Yes." Silently we walked to my car. We didn't speak until we hit the highway.

"What did he say?" Maxi asked.

"He admitted to having an affair with Heather but denied having anything to do with her death."

"You believe him?"

"Yes."

I treated us to chicken salad croissants and lattes at The Fragrant Grind before she drove back to her farm. I had time to do a couple of loads of laundry before I had to go to the bank to see the new cameras being installed.

Uncle Barney was already there, with Clark Bailey. After exchanging greetings, my uncle told me that Fox was almost finished.

I had never met the man and had always assumed that Fox was his last name. After seeing him, I wondered if perhaps it was a nickname. His reddish hair and small, bright eyes gave him a lupine appearance. From the way he responded to Uncle Barney and almost saluted him, I wondered if they'd served in Vietnam together.

When I saw the hanging plants, I coveted them. "They look wonderful. I love them."

"Not bad," Mr. Bailey admitted.

"Good job, Foxy," Barney said.

Fox beamed with pride. "I recommend that you replace the tapes with new ones at the end of the day."

Uncle Barney nodded and turned to me. "Cybil will determine if she needs to watch the tapes."

Fox demonstrated how to load the cameras. He

handed me a gadget that looked a lot like a television remote control. All I had to do to start and stop the camera was to press a button. So far, so good.

Nothing happened on Monday. The flagged dormant accounts remained intact.

It was a long, boring day, checking columns of figures. If this case dragged on, I'd end up cross-eyed and hating numbers.

Uncle Barney checked Sanford Rogers's alibi. The preacher had indeed led a revival meeting on Michigan's Upper Peninsula, which had gone on until close to midnight. Not even flying a plane could he have made it back in time to drop the sleeping pills into Heather's drink. The time of her death, according to Sam, was between ten and midnight.

I took Sanford Rogers's name off the list. He had briefly looked good as a suspect. Oddly enough, I was both sorry and relieved that he was in the clear. I placed the cuff link into a padded envelope and mailed it to the post office box listed on his card.

The one bit of good news was that I could tell Louise that her application had been approved: her daughter could stay at the Hamilton Center for two more weeks. I found her in the break room. Her eyes misted and her voice broke as she thanked me.

"There's no need to thank me. I was glad I could help." That was true. I rarely felt as good as when I could do something nice for someone else.

"I went to visit Stephanie yesterday. Did you know they won't let parents visit for the first three weeks the kids are in the treatment center?"

I nodded. "How is Stephanie?"

"You know, she was actually civil to me. At home she was always so angry. I never knew why, and I guess she didn't either. She asked if Deacon had called. When I told her he hadn't, she looked so down I nearly cried."

"Poor girl. So young to have her heart broken. But being young, she's also resilient. She'll bounce back."

"I'm praying she'll learn from this experience."

So was I, but there was no guarantee that this would happen. Some people learned from experience, others didn't. "The coffee's done. You want a cup?" I asked Louise.

"Yeah, thanks."

I poured two cups and handed her one. "How did she look?"

"Good. Isn't that a funny thing? She looked better than she had when she lived at home. Her color was good and her complexion had cleared up."

"There's lots to be said for regular hours, a balanced diet, and exercise. Not to mention the absence of drugs and alcohol. At the center she has no choice but to live a healthy life."

"Amen," Louise said.

Agnes rushed past us into the bathroom. I was shocked at her pallor. Louise and I exchanged a look.

"Agnes looks sick," I murmured. "Do you know what's wrong with her?"

"It's that miserable boyfriend of hers."

"Did she tell you that?"

"No, but I've known her for a long time. She only gets like this when he's giving her a hard time. Agnes is smart. I can't believe she lets him treat her so bad." Louise sighed.

"What exactly did he do?" I asked, hoping Louise wouldn't think me overly nosy.

"The usual. He goes out drinking with the boys at some bar down by the river."

That struck a familiar chord. "The Last Drop?"

"Yeah. That's the one. You know it?"

"I know of it. I've been told it's not one of our classier joints."

"That's what Agnes said. She doesn't want him to go there, but he does. She suspects the barmaid has designs on him. If it were me, I'd say she was welcome to him. Women can be so dumb when it comes to men."

"There's still too many of us who think we're nothing without a man."

"Isn't that the truth," Louise said, shaking her head.

None of the dormant accounts was accessed the rest of the week. Feeling that I was wasting my time, I phoned Uncle Barney on Friday and asked him to wait for me at the agency. I had to talk to him. Not that he left the agency at five on the dot, but sometimes he had a late afternoon golf game.

Lynn had left for the day when I arrived at the office and for once I was spared her disapproving stares and critical comments. She didn't like me much, but then I didn't think she liked anyone except Uncle Barney, to whom she was fanatically devoted.

"Let me guess," Uncle Barney said. "You feel like you're wasting your time."

"Aren't I? Nothing is happening. You suppose the embezzler guessed about the surveillance cameras?"

"How could she? Only you and Mr. Bailey know about the cameras in the plants. Did you let anything slip?"

"No. Absolutely not."

"And as much as Mr. Bailey invested in the cameras, I'm sure he kept silent also."

"It's just so hard doing nothing but checking transactions that I'm not even sure need to be checked. I wish I were back in a teller's cage. That wasn't boring. I was doing something useful. And the day passed quickly."

"There will be a break in the case. Sooner than later. Patience, Cybil. The embezzler has come to depend on the extra money from the dormant accounts. She'll help herself to some again. I'm sure of that. So hang in there."

That was easier said than done. When Uncle Barney rose, so did I. Time to go home.

Chapter Seven

The first thing I did Saturday morning was mow the lawn. Then I looked at my house, room by room. The dining room was finished and looked great. Since the living room was in the best shape of all the rooms in the house, I decided to leave it till the rest of the downstairs was redone.

On my to-do list was the back parlor, or morning room, which Maxi used when she stayed with me; the bathroom; the kitchen; and the library, which I used as my bedroom. I loved sleeping surrounded by books. Only about a third of the bookcases were filled, which held out the glorious promise of adding books for years and years before I ran out of space.

Luckily, both the bathroom and the kitchen were done in a style that was making a comeback. What goes around comes around, apparently. The deep tub with its claw feet and the white ceramic tiles on the walls and the floor were in good shape. The room needed some color, though. On cold days its vast whiteness made me shiver.

The kitchen needed work. I loved the glass-fronted cabinets, but the white paint had turned yellowish. If I painted the cabinets, the kitchen would look immeasurably better. What color, though?

I showered, dressed in jeans and a T-shirt, and drove to the last of the independently owned hardware stores in town. I loved walking through the narrow, crowded aisles, wondering what the unfamiliar tools were—and most of them were unfamiliar to me.

Standing in front of the gallon cans of paint, I studied the strips of color. I kept going back to the shades of green. Two in particular appealed to me. One reminded me of the green of a willow in spring, the other of the slightly darker green of basil leaves.

While I tried to decide between the colors, I became aware of voices on the other side of the high shelf. I couldn't make out every word, but there was something familiar about the tense voices.

Briefly I debated whether I should walk away and give the speakers privacy. Then I thought I recognized the woman's voice: Agnes. Was it possible? Westport wasn't a big town. I ran into people I knew all the time.

The man's voice said, ". . . chase me down like a . . ."

Agnes: ". . . need it now."

Man: "That much?"

Agnes: "Get it."

Man: ". . . Monday."

Silence. I waited a few beats before I walked around the paint shelf to look into the other aisle. I saw Agnes pick up a can of turpentine and walk toward the check-out counter. I looked around for the man. There were several, but one was obviously with his wife, one had a small boy in tow, and another was with a co-worker, judging by the identical construction company overalls they wore. Where was the man who'd talked with Agnes? I knew he hadn't walked out the front door.

By the time I remembered that there was a side entrance, I suspected he was long gone. Still I hurried toward the other exit. Then it hit me. I didn't know what he looked like. Agnes's friend could be any of the unaccompanied men in the store. Another thing struck me. He hadn't sounded like a friend. There had been an undercurrent of anger and resentment. Odd how emotions in a voice could be detected even if the words were unintelligible.

The man had something Agnes wanted, something he would give her on Monday—reluctantly.

Discouraged, I returned to the paint section, bought what I needed, and drove home.

On Monday I found a dozen reasons to be on the main floor near Agnes's window. Even though I knew that the chances of catching the mystery man in the act of giving Agnes whatever he'd promised were slim to none, I tried to keep an eye on her.

I could, of course, view the security tape from the camera trained on her station after the bank closed. Since none of the dormant accounts had been accessed, I hadn't had to spend hours viewing videotapes yet. Might as well look at one as a practice run.

Fortunately, Monday was a slow day and ten minutes after closing, the night watchman and I were the only ones in the bank. Force of habit made me check the dormant accounts first. I almost fell off the chair when one of them blinked, indicating that it had been opened. Blast. I checked to see how much had been withdrawn and caught my breath. Five thousand dollars. Mr. Bailey was going to have a fit.

I visualized each teller, wondering which one of them needed this much money. None seemed to be living on a scale that required massive amounts of extra cash. Except perhaps Agnes. I had no trouble imagining her boyfriend wheedling and cajoling and sweet-talking her for money.

Lowering the hanging plants and exchanging the tapes the way Foxy had shown me, I took the videos into the break room to view them. Naturally, I chose Agnes's tape first.

Four hours later I realized that I could not get this job done at the bank. I was hungry, I was tired, and I had viewed only a half a day's work of one of the six tellers. Five, actually, as Heather's replacement was too new to come under suspicion.

I phoned Uncle Barney at his house and told him what had happened.

"What do you want to do?" he asked.

"Take the tapes home and look at them there tomorrow. I'll call in sick."

"That's a good idea. I could send Glenn to help you—"

"He wouldn't know what to look for. I need to do this." Uncle Barney was silent. I could picture him fiddling with his pipe while he considered my plan.

"You're right. You have to look at the tapes. And it'll be tedious. As tedious as sitting in a car for hours doing surveillance."

"I realize that," I said, trying not to sound discouraged.

"Let me know as soon as you spot something."

Promising that I would, I took the tapes and drove toward Westport. On the way I stopped at the Far East Restaurant for a carryout order of moo shu chicken. I had no time to cook.

Viewing the second half of Agnes's tape, it occurred to me that I could fast forward the segments where she actually dealt with customers. She wouldn't have time to access a dormant account while transacting legitimate banking business. She had to do it during a banking lull. That sped things up a bit. As did the fact that she closed her window for an hour, presumably to work at other tasks that her position as assistant head teller demanded.

I finished viewing her tape at midnight. My eyes burned, my head hurt, and my bottom felt numb from sitting still so long. Worse, I had spotted nothing illegal going on. My vaunted intuition had led me down the garden path. Disappointed, I fell into bed and for once fell asleep immediately.

At seven the next morning, I brewed a pot of strong coffee, toasted an English muffin, slathered it with strawberry preserves, and watched the next video. Carol spent a lot of time doodling on a piece of paper when she had no customers. Ninety minutes later, Agnes, carrying her cash drawer, came to take over for her as Carol went on break.

How could I have forgotten that the tellers spelled each other for breaks and for lunch? I watched Agnes closely, but suddenly there was a rush of customers so that she couldn't have withdrawn money even if she had wanted to.

I tried to remember which teller's place Agnes had taken at lunch and for the afternoon break, but I couldn't. Of all the tellers, I was closest to Louise. How odd would she think it was if I phoned her and asked her if Agnes had taken her place? It didn't matter how odd. I needed the information.

"Louise, this is Cybil. Are you alone in the break room?"

"Yeah. Why?"

"Did Agnes spell you for lunch or afternoon break yesterday?"

"No, Susan did. Agnes took over for Millie, the new teller. Why?"

"I was checking something. It's nothing. Thanks." I hung up before she could ask more questions.

I popped Millie's tape into the VCR and fast-forwarded it to the place where Agnes took over. She helped two customers. Then I saw her reach for the withdrawal slips. Calmly she filled in the form, accessed the account which I was willing to bet was dormant, counted out a handful of bills, divided them into two stacks, and slipped them into the pockets of her skirt. The whole procedure had taken only a couple of minutes. Stunned, I rewound the tape and watched it again.

I reached for the phone. "Lynn, please let me speak to my uncle."

"Is it business-related?" she asked primly.

"Yes."

Moments later, I said, "I caught her."

"Good job. Bring the tape."

"Slick. Very slick. The woman has nerves of steel," Uncle Barney said with grudging admiration.

"Doesn't she, though? She barely glanced at the tellers on either side of her before she broke into the account. And to put fistsful of dollars into her pockets and walk around with it as if this were the most natural thing in the world?" I shook my head. "I could never be that cold-blooded."

"I assume she took the bills in large denominations."

"She must have. Five thousand dollars in twenties would have been too bulky to fit into her pockets."

Uncle Barney nodded. "Your job at the bank is finished."

Shocked, I realized that officially that was true.

"What?" he asked. "I thought you'd be pleased. No more boring columns of figures to check."

"True, but Heather's death hasn't been cleared up."

"That's not our job."

"Then whose is it? The sheriff's? He's satisfied that she committed suicide. There's no one else but us. If we don't solve it, her killer will go free." I stopped to moderate the emotion in my voice. "I know it would bother you if that were to happen."

Uncle Barney rose and paced. "We have to let Mr. Bailey know that we've found the embezzler. Not to do so would be unethical. But I could ask if you could stay a few extra days at the bank. Say the rest of the week. At no cost to the bank."

"I can survive without a week's pay," I said, though I knew it would be difficult, my finances being what they were. The house improvements, even though I was doing many myself, swallowed every spare dollar.

"No, the agency will pay you. We'll absorb the cost."

"I can't let you do that, Uncle Barney."

"Of course you can."

"Lynn will have a hissy fit—"

"Cybil, I run this office. Lynn has nothing to say about this. Well, she probably will have *something* to say, knowing her, but ignore it."

A faint smile tugged at the corners of his mouth. I don't think I ever liked him more than I did at that moment.

Mr. Bailey was stunned when I showed him the video clip.

"I can't believe it's Agnes. She's the last person I'd have suspected. She's been a trusted employee in this bank for more than twenty years. Why? Why did she do it?"

He took Agnes's embezzling as a personal betrayal. I felt compassion for him and decided to tell him the truth.

"Agnes fell in love with a man. A man who isn't very nice and not worthy of her. To help him and to keep him, she decided to take money from the dormant accounts." I told him about Rafe and his racing aspirations.

He sighed and shook his head. "It always comes down to love and money."

I thought maybe sex and money was a more accurate description but didn't say so.

"What will you do?" I asked.

"What choice do I have? None. I have to fire her and make sure she can't get another job in banking."

I was glad he wasn't going to prosecute Agnes.

He yelled for Elaine to come in. "Get Joan Bower on the phone, and after I talk with her, get Agnes up here, please."

"She didn't come in today."

"Did she call in sick?"

"No. She didn't call at all."

"Did you try calling her?"

"Yes. All I got was the machine."

"Not again," I exclaimed before I could stop myself. Mr. Bailey and I looked at each other, obviously fearing the same thing. "I'm driving to her house. She could be sick. Too sick to answer the phone." I saw Mr. Bailey nod on my way to the door.

All the way to her house I kept telling myself that she was okay. She might have gone off with Rafe. As crazy about him as she was, she just might have blown work off.

Her house was a tidy, wooden-frame, story-and-a-half house with a fenced back yard. I heard the dog's barking before I rang the bell. I counted to thirty and rang again. The dog's barking grew more frantic. I looked through the small glass window in the door. For all his fierce barking, the dog was small.

"Agnes, it's Cybil from the bank. Are you in there?" No answer. I walked toward the garage. Through a side window I saw her car. That wasn't good. I walked to the back of the house and knocked on the door. The dog seemed to hurl himself against the door, barking continuously.

I knocked again and called. No answer. Getting seriously alarmed, I looked around. Most people hid a house key somewhere in case they locked themselves out. I checked the welcome mat, the flowerpots, and every object on the back porch. I finally found it taped under the bird feeder.

Now all I had to worry about was the dog. In a singsong voice I said, "Good dog. Good dog, Hiram. You're such a fine little dog." The longer I talked, the calmer the dog got.

I unlocked the door. "Good dog, Hiram. Where's Agnes?" He ran down the hall, hunkered down, and whimpered. My stomach lurched. This was bad.

Now I had to search the house. I walked to the front. The living room to my left was empty, as was the bedroom to my right. I guessed that this room had been her mother's, judging by the family photographs displayed on every available surface. There was no one in the dining room. I turned toward the bedroom across from it.

I knocked on the door and listened. All I could hear were Hiram's whimpers. "Agnes? Are you in there? This is Cybil. I'm coming in." I opened the door, feeling a sense of deja vu.

Agnes lay sprawled across the bed, her right arm dangling toward the floor, motionless. My gaze reached her face. I heard moans, pitiful moans that wouldn't stop. When I realized the moans were mine, I scooped up the dog and slammed the bedroom door shut behind us. I rushed out the back door and collapsed onto the porch floor. I held Hiram. I don't know which one of us shivered more violently.

It seemed to take forever before my hands stopped trembling enough that I could use my cell phone.

"Uncle Barney, please."

"Is this business-related?" Lynn asked.

"Yes," I whispered.

"What's wrong with you?"

"Just let me speak to my uncle." I waited and shivered.

"Cybil, what's wrong?" he asked.

"She's dead."

"Who is dead?"

"Agnes."

"Where?"

"In her bedroom."

"Give me the address of her house."

I did.

"Are you sure she's dead?"

"Yes. She . . . I've never seen anyone who's been strangled, but. . . ." My voice trailed off. My stomach heaved.

"Have you phoned the police?"

"No."

"I'll call Sam. Are you in the house?"

"On the back porch."

"Good. Stay put. I'll be there as fast as I can. Before the police get there."

*   *   *

True to his word, Uncle Barney arrived before the first patrol car did. He sat on the porch step beside me and held my hand.

"I'm going to take a look and then I'll be back."

"It's the second door on your left," I murmured.

He petted Hiram's head and walked toward the door. He used his handkerchief when he touched the doorknob. I hadn't thought of doing that.

When he came back, he carried the dog's leash. "Here, boy," he said and clipped the leash to Hiram's collar. "Safer this way. Soon all sorts of people will be milling around. He might get scared. Let's sit on the lawn chairs, out of the way."

Uncle Barney's voice was soothing. Obediently I followed him to the chairs, which were grouped around a small metal table. He handed me the leash. Hiram sat beside my chair

Sam and his partner arrived just as the first patrol car did. Uncle Barney went into the house with them. I petted Hiram to soothe him. After a while the dog got up and moved toward the house.

"No, Hiram. We can't go inside." Then I noticed a water bowl next to the porch steps. I located a water faucet, filled the bowl, and let Hiram drink. He lapped water for a long time. I berated myself for not guessing he might be thirsty. He was probably hungry too, but I couldn't bring myself to go inside. Besides, Sam would probably tell me to get out.

The sun was warm enough for Hiram to move under

my chair, but I didn't feel warm. If I didn't concentrate hard, I would probably shiver. What I really wanted to do was curl up into a ball, close my eyes, and escape into sleep.

Sam approached and sat in a chair. He took out his notebook and pen.

"Cybil, tell me exactly what happened."

Uncle Barney sat in the other chair and gave me an encouraging nod.

I told Sam about the embezzling.

"And when you arrived here both the front and the back door were locked?"

"Yes. I looked for the key and found it taped to the bird feeder."

"Maybe whoever strangled Agnes found it there, unlocked the door, and later taped the key back in its hiding place," Sam speculated.

"You can't be serious, Sam. The murderer was going to take time to hide the key just after he strangled a woman?" I asked, my voice shocked.

Sam shrugged. "Could have. Nothing surprises me any more."

"Isn't it more likely that Agnes let him inside? Or her?" I asked.

"Him. Agnes was a good-sized woman. It took strength to strangle her."

Despite the tight control I had over myself, a tiny moan of distress escaped my mouth. I bit my lip. Uncle Barney reached out and laid his hand on mine.

"If she let him in, she knew him," Uncle Barney said.

"She probably did," Sam agreed. "Her purse was on the chair with eighty-seven dollars and change in it. Plus a couple of major credit cards. And a television and VCR. The motive probably wasn't robbery."

Uncle Barney and I exchanged a quick look, which didn't escape Sam.

"What?"

"There should have been five thousand dollars in cash. That's how much she embezzled yesterday."

Sam let out a low whistle. He got up and told the officers and his partner to do another, more thorough search. "Not that I'm holding out much hope that we'll find the cash. Five thousand is a tidy motive for murder."

"But who would have known that she had that much cash?" I wondered out loud.

"The person she embezzled it for," Uncle Barney said.

"And who would that be?" Sam asked.

"Her boyfriend," I said. "But he wouldn't murder her. That would be like killing the goose who lays the golden eggs."

"What's the name of this boyfriend?" Sam asked.

"Rafe Carson."

"Any idea where he lives?"

I shook my head.

"You know what he does for a living?"

"As little as possible," I muttered. "At least that's the

impression I got. He races cars on Friday nights at the track west of town."

"Shouldn't be too hard to find him. Anything else you know about him?" Sam asked.

"No."

"What about Agnes? Who's her next of kin?"

I tried to recall the personal information in her folder. "She has a sister in Chicago. The bank has the address. I don't think there's anyone else. Except Hiram here." I leaned down and petted him.

"Cute little fellow. I'll have one of the guys take him to the animal shelter," Sam said.

"No!" My vehement tone surprised both men. "He's not going to the shelter. If no one adopts him, he'll . . ." To my chagrin, my voice broke. With a supreme effort I suppressed the tears that lodged in my throat and burned like fire. I wouldn't let myself fall apart. I couldn't allow myself to cry. If I did, I wasn't sure when I'd stop. Mercifully, neither man made a comment. They both stared at their feet, as if they felt rather uncomfortable. When I had myself under control, I said, "I'll take him home with me. Any objections?"

"No. As long as I know where he is. In case the sister wants him. Though why she would, I don't know. He's just a mutt. You know, the kind whose daddy was a traveling man and his mama the town's shady lady."

"Sam! That's a terrible thing to say about him. What if he understood you?" I knew it was illogical, but I wanted to cover Hiram's ears to protect him.

"Just trying to lighten the mood," Sam said. "Besides, I said he was cute."

"Cybil has been through a lot today. Can we leave?" Uncle Barney asked.

"Yeah, if Cybil doesn't remember anything else."

"I don't."

"If you do, you know where to find me. Take it easy, Cybil."

"Can you drive, or do you want to ride with me? I can send someone to pick up your car."

"I can drive. Can I go home for a while?"

He nodded. "I'll follow you."

"Will you tell Mr. Bailey at the bank what happened?"

"Of course I will, Cybil," Uncle Barney said.

Chapter Eight

At my house Uncle Barney put the tea kettle on. He rummaged through the cupboards until he found a box of mint tea bags, then sweetened my cup with a spoonful of honey. Then he telephoned the bank.

I motioned for him to hand me the phone before he hung up. "Hold on, Mr. Bailey. Cybil wants to talk to you."

Taking the phone, I said, "I'm so sorry. I seem to be the one who keeps bringing you bad news."

"It's not your fault," he said, his voice shaky.

"I know it's a lot to ask you right now, but before you tell the staff what happened, could you do me a favor?"

"Of course."

"Could you empty Agnes's locker without telling anyone and keep her things locked up until I have a chance to look at them, please?" A lengthy silence followed my request. "I know this will be difficult, but it's important."

"All right," he agreed reluctantly.

"Thank you. I'll be in later today. If not, then first thing in the morning." I hung up.

"Are you sure you'll be up to going to the bank?"

"I don't know. But I need to look at the contents of her locker." I placed my hands around the mug to warm them. "Who'd do such a thing?" I wondered out loud. I took a sip of the fragrant, sweet tea, which had a restorative effect on my spirits.

"Somebody who had a lot to lose. Somebody who panicked."

"What could Agnes have known or done that would have driven someone to such a desperate act?"

"It could be something that to us would seem insignificant, but to the killer it was a big deal. Something that threatened him. Threatened his survival, his possessions, his good name, or his sense of self-worth."

I had only thought in terms of tangible things, but Uncle Barney was right. Loss of reputation and self-worth could be incredibly damaging.

"We, at least I, need to take a look at Agnes's house. There's got to be something there to give us a clue."

Uncle Barney shook his head. "The house is now a crime scene. It'll be a couple of days before Sam will let anyone go inside."

I had kept the house key. I had meant to put it back under the bird feeder, but after finding Agnes's body, I'd forgotten all about it and Sam hadn't asked me for it. He probably took the key that had hung by the back door, next to Agnes's car keys. Getting into the house would be no problem, but if Sam caught me, there'd be the devil to pay, even if the criminal investigation was finished.

But what were the chances that Sam would go back to the house? I was sure he and his men had done a thorough job already.

"Will you ask Sam when we—no, better say—when the bank can get into the house?"

"What do you think you might find in the house?" Uncle Barney asked.

"I don't know. Maybe nothing. But I have to look." My intuition fairly screamed at me to go there. I got up and paced, too restless to sit. "Two tellers of a branch bank have been murdered. Surely now no one still thinks that Heather committed suicide? The deaths have to be connected."

"You told me that Heather lived above her means. She could have been embezzling from the dormant accounts too."

"True." I thought about that for a moment. "But that couldn't be a motive for murder. It's the bank's money. Why would Heather particularly care if Agnes took it, or vice versa? The motive has to be something more personal."

"I think you're right." Uncle Barney rose. "I better

get back to the agency. You're sure you don't want me to phone Luke?"

"I'm sure." There was nothing Luke could do to erase the image of Agnes's body from my mind. I shuddered. I'd have to learn to live with it.

To distract myself, I changed my clothes and painted a couple of kitchen cabinets.

Then I took Hiram for a walk around the neighborhood. He had a good time sniffing out the new territory.

By five o'clock I couldn't stand it anymore. I had to go to the bank and look at the contents of Agnes's locker. I phoned Mr. Bailey, who promised to wait for me.

He brought the carton from the safe and set it on my desk.

"There wasn't all that much, but maybe something's already missing."

"How could that be?" I asked with a frown.

"Her locker was open. Unless she forgot to lock it, but that doesn't sound like Agnes."

"No, it doesn't. She wasn't careless or flighty or forgetful." How could anyone have gained access to her locker? Agnes wasn't the chummy type who'd share her combination. Then I remembered that the combinations were kept in the small vault upstairs, whose doors I'd seen standing open several times. Anybody could have gotten the locker combination.

I looked through her stuff. Unlike Heather, she kept no clothes in her locker. A toothbrush and a tube of toothpaste, hand lotion, a pair of sunglasses, a box of tea bags and packages of sweetener, an envelope of photos. And a small framed photo of Hiram.

Since Mr. Bailey seemed eager to leave, I took the photographs. "I'll look at these at home and bring them back tomorrow." He had no objection to that.

Maxi had a key to my house. She was waiting for me in the kitchen, Hiram sitting at her feet.

"What a darling dog. Whose is he?" she asked.

I told her about Agnes.

"How awful for you to find her like that. And the poor dog. How dreadful for him." She petted him, murmuring comforting words. Hiram was lapping it up, his tail thumping the floor. "What will happen to him?"

"I'm not sure. Sam wanted to take him to the animal shelter, but I wouldn't let him. Hiram needs a good home." I looked at Maxi. Casually, I added, "He's a great watchdog. He started to bark before I even set foot on the porch."

"Such a good little dog," Maxi cooed, still stroking his fur.

"He's well-mannered. And already house-broken. He'd be no problem at all."

"I'd take him in a heartbeat, but I'm seventy-five. He could be orphaned again."

That stabbed me to the heart. I couldn't bear to think of losing Maxi. Quickly, I said, "I promise if that were to happen, which it isn't, I'll take him and take care of him."

"In that case, Hiram, would you like to go home with me?"

I swear Hiram nodded. I knew he couldn't have, but I thought he had. The two were made for each other.

"I brought supper," she said.

"How lovely. What did you bring?"

"*Rouladen.*"

"My favorite. I'll make mashed potatoes to go with them," I offered. The thinly sliced steaks were stuffed, browned, and simmered in a delicious gravy.

"Oma, do you want to feed Hiram? I brought his bowls and the bag of dog food. There's a plastic cup in the bag so I assume he gets a cupful of the dry food."

"All right." Maxi read the information on the bag. "Cybil, put the kettle on, please. It says here the food tastes better if hot water is poured on it to make a gravy. Of course, we could also put a little of the *Rouladen* gravy on it."

"Listen to you. He isn't even at your house yet and already you're spoiling him," I said, my tone teasing.

"A little spoiling won't hurt him, especially after what he's been through."

"I wish he could talk. I'm sure he saw the killer."

"You don't suppose he actually witnessed—"

"No. I'm sure Hiram would have attacked the killer if he'd seen him hurt Agnes."

"How do you know he didn't?"

That stopped me cold. "I don't." I reached for the phone and dialed. Sam was still at the police station.

"Maxi and I were talking and it occurred to us that Hiram may have bitten the killer. He may be small, but he's feisty. He's protective and can be ferocious." I heard what I suspected might have been a smothered chuckle.

"You want me to have one of my men call all the doctors and ask if they treated a dog bite wound yesterday? A wound inflicted by a scruffy little ankle biter?"

"He's not a scruffy little ankle biter, and it's not a bad idea," I said defensively.

"No, not if I had unlimited manpower," he said and hung up.

"He didn't think much of the idea?" Maxi asked.

"He doesn't have the manpower."

"Hmm."

I looked at Maxi suspiciously. "Whenever you make that thoughtful *hmm* sound, you're up to something. What?"

"Nothing, *Schatzi*."

The tea kettle whistled and suddenly Maxi was very busy with Hiram and I got busy with the potatoes. Though I didn't buy her innocent *nothing, Schatzi*, I dropped the subject and concentrated on preparing dinner.

While we ate, both of us were silent. Finally Maxi said, "I don't mean to be ghoulish, but I can't stop thinking about Agnes."

"Me neither," I admitted.

"You must suspect somebody. I mean, Agnes didn't live in a vacuum."

"I keep wondering about her boyfriend."

"Tell me about him."

"He's very good-looking and very aware of it. He's at least fifteen years younger than Agnes. And she was totally crazy about him."

"Oh dear. That's a prescription for disaster. Or at least great unhappiness."

I nodded. "I'm sure he pressured her into financing his racing. And to do that, she embezzled money."

"Oh my. How much?"

"That's hard to say, but I estimate a hundred thousand or so. She took fifteen thousand dollars in the short time I've been at the bank."

Maxi put her fork down. "She would have gone to prison for quite a few years, wouldn't she?"

"Yes, but Mr. Bailey wouldn't have pressed charges. She would have lost her job, though, her insurance benefits, and maybe even her pension. She'd worked at the bank for twenty-plus years."

"She risked all that for a man." Maxi sighed and shook her head.

"I could be wrong, but I had the feeling that this was her first and only great love and she was willing to go the all-or-nothing route."

"And she did. She risked all and lost all. I have to

admire that a little." Maxi paused. "You know I don't usually encourage you to go after criminals, but you have to find her killer. I'll help you. What can I do?"

"What you've already decided to do," I said with a knowing look. "Canvass the doctors to see if any of them treated a dog bite wound yesterday or maybe today. He could have put off going until today."

"I can do that."

"Maybe you'd better talk to the receptionists. They'll be more approachable. You'll have to come up with a convincing story as to why you need to know that."

"I'll take Hiram along. I'll say that the neighbor's kids thought he had bitten some man who came into my yard. I just want to make sure the man gets treatment if that happened. I want to avoid a lawsuit. What do you think?"

"Sounds plausible. You're a good actress, Oma."

She grinned. "I know. I'm especially good at playing dithering old ladies."

"You're so bad," I said, grinning back at her.

After Maxi and Hiram left, I looked at the photographs from Agnes's locker. Most of them were taken at the race track, featuring Rafe, who looked great in his silver racing outfit. No clues in any of them. At least none that I could see. The framed photo of Hiram looked as if it might have been taken by a professional. The dog looked adorable, his little head cocked slightly to the left. I set it on the small television set I kept in the kitchen.

I wandered aimlessly around my house until I reached a decision. Even if Sam threw me in jail for the night, I had to search Agnes's house.

I changed my clothes. Wearing black jeans, a long-sleeved dark gray T-shirt and sneakers, my longish hair stuffed under a baseball cap, I felt ready to join Cary Grant on the steep rooftops of Monte Carlo and do a little second-story work.

When I got to Agnes's house, it was almost dark. Holding the flashlight in one hand, I fumbled for the key in my pocket. From the corner of my eye I caught movement. I grabbed the pole that held the bird feeder, intending to use it as a weapon if necessary.

"Who's there?" I demanded, shining the flashlight at the figure. "Rafe? What are you doing here?"

"I could ask you the same thing," he said, stepping out of the shadows.

"I'm here from the bank," I lied brazenly.

"And I'm here to pick up some stuff I left here."

I thought he was lying as brazenly as I was. "You better come back in a couple of days. This is still considered a crime scene." Then it hit me. "How did you know Agnes was dead?"

"The cops came to see me."

"Oh. I'm sorry about Agnes. I know you were . . . friends."

"Yeah. She was a good egg."

A good egg? Not exactly a romantic endearment, but then I'd suspected all along that her love was rather one-sided. "She cared about you."

"I know, and I appreciated it."

"What did the cops say?"

"Not much after they checked my alibi."

"Which was?"

"I spent the whole day and night with someone."

"A woman?"

"Yes, if you must know. And why are you asking so many questions?"

It had taken him long enough to wonder about that. "I worked with Agnes. I want whoever did this to her punished."

"Me too. She helped me with my racecar. I'd never have hurt her." He turned away. "You can believe that or not, but it's the truth." Rafe walked toward the alley.

I watched him disappear into the darkness. No, it wouldn't make sense for him to kill his sponsor. Unless she got tired of shelling out money. And she would have stopped supporting him if she found out about his other woman. Or, more likely, other women. Had Agnes found out? Had she threatened to drop him? Had they argued? Had the argument gotten out of hand?

As far as I was concerned, Rafe was still a candidate for murder, alibi notwithstanding. How hard would it be for him to get a woman to lie? He'd gotten one to steal for him and risk going to prison. Lying would be easy.

I slipped my hands into the latex gloves I'd brought, unlocked the back door, and entered the house. I considered turning on a light but decided against it. No one was supposed to be in the house. Any passing patrol car spotting the light would stop and investigate.

Using the flashlight, I oriented myself. The hall ran straight from the back door to the front door, dividing the house down the middle. On my right was the kitchen, then the dining room with the living room facing the street. On my immediate left was a laundry room, then a bathroom and two bedrooms. Not a big house but big enough to offer many hiding places.

The house felt hot and stuffy. I could feel perspiration dampen my forehead. I opened the window in the laundry room, reminding myself to close it before I left.

I did a quick walk-through. Agnes had kept a tidy house. Some of the furniture was old. It had probably been her mother's or even her grandmother's, but it had that polished, well-taken-care-of look.

In the front bedroom, which I suspected had been her mother's, I saw neatly arranged photo albums. At some point I'd look through them. Finishing my walk-through, I ended up at the back door. I might as well start with the kitchen.

Agnes's kitchen was well stocked. The woman had

done some serious cooking. For Rafe? I hoped so. I hoped she'd been happy, preparing meals for her man. I shone my flashlight over the cupboards, the drawers, the canisters lined up in military order on the counter and conceded defeat. This was a daylight job. Holding a flashlight with one hand while searching the drawers would take too long. This was not only a daylight job but also a two-handed task.

Since I didn't know what I was looking for, I didn't know where I should begin. I asked myself some questions. Were both women killed by the same person? Probably. Even though one was poisoned, which suggested a logical, carefully worked-out plan, and the other strangled, which suggested fury, passion, heat of the moment, loss of control.

What did Heather and Agnes have in common? Heather was young, impulsive, spoiled, and liked men who could spend lots of money on her. Agnes was older, intense, passionate, and spent lots of money on one man—money she had stolen for him.

It seemed to me that the most telling thing they shared was friendship and their place of employment: the bank. Had Heather discovered Agnes's embezzling? If so, did she want a cut? Did she threaten to expose Agnes? Theoretically I could make a somewhat plausible case that Agnes poisoned Heather. But then who killed Agnes and why? No matter how long I stood in Agnes's hallway and argued with myself, I always ended up with the conclusion that the same person had killed both women. I just didn't know why or who. Yet.

Did my arguments eliminate Rafe as a suspect? Had he known Heather? He could have. And fancying himself a ladies' man, did he make a pass at Heather? Had Agnes found out and. . . . That was weak. I shook my head. Although Rafe might not have been the faithful type, as long as Agnes gave him money, he would have been at least discreet.

All these what-ifs got me nowhere. I might as well tackle the bedrooms. That's when I heard the noise. From the front of the house. I froze until I heard it again. A key being inserted. I had to get out of the house. I did not want another dunking in the lake.

Too late. I heard the door swing open and then close with a cautious click. The intruder seemed to have stopped just inside the door. I had to hide. Silently I crept toward the door that connected the kitchen with the dining room. On my walk-through I'd seen the large dining room table, which dominated the middle of the room. I crawled under it. The lace tablecloth reached halfway to the floor. The chairs were pushed under the table, creating a fairly good hiding place.

Listening to the footsteps, I tried to gauge the intruder's progress through the hall. By the heaviness of his steps, I guessed it was a man. He seemed to pause at each door. When he stopped in the dining room doorway, I held my breath. I watched the beam of the flashlight play over the room. What had seemed like an excellent hiding place now looked like a trap.

A lifetime later, he moved on. I breathed again, carefully, silently, not daring to gasp air into my burning lungs. He continued down the hall. Would he notice the open window? Would he wonder if someone else was in the house? I had left my car in the parking lot of the convenience store two blocks down the street. Other than the open window, he had no reason to suspect he wasn't the only intruder.

Apparently the window didn't alarm him, for he walked into one of the two bedrooms across the hall. I couldn't be sure which one. I had no way of tracking time, but I thought I crouched under that table for a short eternity. I heard small noises, suggesting he was looking for something.

The house had seemed hot and stuffy before, but under the table, the heat was overpowering. Not daring to make any noise, not even the faint whisper of blotting my face with my T-shirt, I let the sweat drip down my face. Dazed by heat and half-paralyzed by fear, I thought perhaps this was a foretaste of purgatory.

While I hunkered down, I wondered if I could make it to the back door without him catching me. I doubted it. Better to sit tight.

Finally, finally, I heard him come out of the room and walk toward the front of the house. When I heard him go out and close the door behind him, I crawled out from my hiding place. Though my impulse was to run like the wind out the back door, I had to look out the window even though it was unlikely he had parked in front of the house. He hadn't.

But I did hear a car start down the block. Ducking low, I darted outside and pressed myself against the large oak in front of the house. I saw car lights and a vehicle pulling into the street. From the shape I saw fleetingly, it was some sort of sports utility vehicle.

I hurried back inside and moved as quickly as I could toward the back of the house. I slipped out, closed the door behind me, and took off running through the alley. When I reached the street I heard the siren of a police car. Fear shot through me. Were the cops after me? Technically, I was probably guilty of breaking and entering, but how did they know?

I forced myself to slow down to a walk. The black-and-white car streaked down the street, its lights flashing. The two teenagers walking past me talked about the accident that had just happened down the block. Thank heaven the cops weren't after me. I kept going.

When I saw the lights of the convenience store, my breathing returned to near normal. With trembling hands I unlocked my car to get my purse. In the store I bought two bottles of water, one of which I drank as I waited in line to pay.

Without staring inquisitively, I examined the customers in the store. None of them seemed to possess the shape of the intruder as I had formed it in my mind. Besides, why would he come to this convenience store?

Was I getting paranoid? I hoped not, but I didn't linger in the store.

At my house, I parked in front rather than driving through the alley that led to my garage. I wanted to get inside quickly and lock the door behind me and feel safe.

In the dim light shed by the lamps flanking the porch, I saw the figure of a man sitting on the steps. Luke. I was in no mood for explanations and confrontations. What I wanted was a shower and gallons of something cold to drink. But Luke had seen me. I had no choice but to go inside.

"Hi, Luke," I managed to say calmly.

"Cybil."

He didn't say anything else until we were inside.

"Maxi phoned me and told me about her new pet."

"Yes, she and Hiram took to one another. And living on a farm, she really should have a dog. She used to have dogs."

"I remember one who was part collie," Luke said.

"Waldie. He was a great pet."

Walking toward the kitchen, I asked, "You want some juice? A soft drink?"

"I'll have what you have."

I poured two glasses of vegetable juice. I drained mine and refilled my glass. I felt the need for vitamin C, now that the adrenaline high was draining from my body. I took a deep breath, willing my hands not to start shaking.

"You're breathless," Luke observed. "What have you been up to?"

"Running."

His left eyebrow lifted. He studied me with dark, intense eyes. "You don't like to run. You don't even like to jog."

"True. But sometimes you've no choice." As soon as I said this, I knew it had been a mistake.

"You've been doing something you weren't supposed to be doing. I know your guilty look, Cybil."

No use lying. Luke knew me too well.

"I drove past Agnes's house."

"Isn't that still a crime scene?"

"I'm not sure. Driving past isn't illegal."

"No, not if that's all you did. What happened?"

"I got strange vibes. They made me nervous."

"I've never known you to be superstitious."

Shrugging, I ignored his statement. "Was there a specific reason you came to see me?"

"Yes. I wondered if you might want to go sailing with me. I thought you enjoyed yourself last time."

"I did. And yes, I'd like to go again."

"Good. Sometime over the Memorial Day weekend?"

"Fine."

"The schedule isn't up yet so I don't know exactly when I'll be off-duty."

"Let me know when you can." I walked Luke to the front door.

"Cybil, did you agree to go sailing to get rid of me? I feel like I'm getting the bum's rush."

"Hardly. You know I'm perfectly capable of saying no."

He looked at me searchingly. Then he said, "I'll be in touch."

"Good night, Luke." I locked the door behind him and collapsed on the bottom step of the staircase.

He hadn't been entirely wrong about the bum's rush. I needed to decompress, to process what had happened, but I couldn't confide in him. It would reinforce all his prejudices against my job.

Could I, should I, tell Uncle Barney? Probably not. I had slipped under the yellow crime scene tape, which was clearly meant to keep everyone out. Entering a crime scene was probably a misdemeanor, if not a felony. I couldn't involve anyone else.

So far I was the only one who knew that I had been in the house with Agnes's killer. At least I was almost dead certain the intruder had been the murderer. Who else would come to search it? There had to be something incriminating in the house.

I'd have to go back. Tomorrow. Nothing could induce me to go back there tonight.

Of course, if the killer had found what he was looking for, I was out of luck. Still, I had to make sure.

Chapter Nine

After a night of restless sleep, I got up early and brewed a pot of coffee. My head felt thick, even though I hadn't had anything to drink the night before except a six-pack of V8 juice. When the coffee was done, I poured myself a cup.

I took the shorthand notebook from my shoulder bag and opened it to a new page. What did I need to do? First, check to see if anyone else had accessed the dormant accounts. Unlikely. Or was it? Check to be sure.

Rafe Carson. Could he be Agnes's killer? I hated to think so, but I should take another look at him. Had he been last night's intruder? He had freely admitted that there were things in the house he wanted. But the police had cleared him. They would allow him to retrieve his stuff in a few days. No need to risk a breaking and entering charge. Besides, Rafe was young and moved with the quick, lithe steps of a young man. Last night's intruder had moved more slowly, heavily.

Who else was there in Agnes's life who could have a reason for wanting her dead? The people at the bank? I visualized them: Louise, eternally dieting; Carol, long-suffering; Susan, forever whining; Edward, prissy, gossipy; Mr. Bailey, worried, bewildered. Hardly a rogue's lineup. And yet . . .

I closed my notebook. Making lists did not help me. Maybe because I thought logically to begin with? Whatever. I might as well go to work.

Edward pounced on me the moment I set foot in the bank. He accompanied me upstairs. I slowed my pace to accommodate his limp.

"Any news on Agnes?" he asked.

"What kind of news?"

"Well, anything. Who and how she was killed, for starters."

"It takes several days for an autopsy to be done."

"You know that lieutenant cop, don't you? Sam Keller? What does he say?"

"I may know Sam, but that doesn't mean he confides in me."

"You found Agnes. You saw her."

"Yes, but I'm not a physician. From what I saw, let's just say she didn't die of natural causes."

Edward went into his shrugging-squinting routine, making me squirm.

"Agnes, of all people, to get herself murdered. If I were the police, I'd look real close at that boyfriend of hers."

"Why?"

"Isn't it obvious?"

"Not to me," I said.

"He's a very young, very good-looking guy, half her age. And Agnes . . . well, not to speak ill of the dead, but she was a bit of a stick-in-the-mud."

Why was it when people said they weren't going to speak ill of the dead, they invariably did?

"She was a nice enough person, but hardly a woman a young, dashing racer would be looking for. Heather would have been more his type."

I stopped at the top of the stairs and faced him. I couldn't help but defend Agnes. "You're wrong. I'm sure Heather and Rafe found each other attractive, but neither met the other's needs."

Edward frowned. "I don't understand what you mean."

"Heather had no family. It's no accident that she dated older men almost exclusively. And it wasn't just because they had money. She needed a father figure."

"What about Rafe? He could have any of the young things at the track."

"I'm sure he could, and I'm sure he had his share,

but Agnes brought stability and order to his life. She was an anchor for him."

"Not to mention his financier." Edward smirked. Then he added, "I would have thought an anchor, something to hold him down and back, was the last thing Rafe wanted."

"Everyone needs someone or something to anchor them. Otherwise they get sucked under by the moral chaos and senseless randomness that surrounds us."

Edward did one of his shrugging things, making me look at the far wall.

"You have a funny way of looking at life," he said and limped toward Elaine's desk.

By funny I guessed he didn't mean "ha-ha" funny, but odd. My view of life was a fairly standard one, which made me wonder what his was. Again, I felt that there was something a little off-center about Edward, and it wasn't just his physical quirks. I tried to summon up the tolerance Maxi had worked so hard to instill in me.

After checking my mail, I went back downstairs. I used the teller's cage that had the CLOSED sign in the window. Mr. Bailey would be looking for another teller. Or rather, as soon as he saw me, he'd assign that task to me. I accessed the flagged accounts just as a matter of form. I didn't think any of them would have been plundered. I did a classic double take when I saw the blinking light.

Muttering a few silent curses, I checked to see how much had been withdrawn. Five thousand. Blast. I hurried upstairs to inform Mr. Bailey. The poor man looked as if he wanted to cry when I told him.

"Am I sitting in the middle of a nest of vipers? Is everyone in this bank a thief? Do I have to fire the whole darn bunch of them and start from scratch?"

I let him rant and vent for a while. Then I said, "I'll watch the videotapes tonight." That wasn't something I was looking forward to.

"I sure hope the agency pays you overtime."

"No, but we get comp time. I could use a day off to work in my garden. The weeds grow faster than the flowers."

"Don't they always."

Since the bank was short-handed, I went downstairs to spell Carol. Looking at her closely, I couldn't detect the tell-tale heavy makeup used to conceal bruises. Had she embezzled five thousand dollars to keep her husband in drinking money?

As always, Susan told me all about her daily domestic woes from the dryer with the broken belt, to her whining mother-in-law, to her son's latest therapy, which was expensive but going well. That ought to have cheered her up enough to make all other problems appear trivial, but I guess she needed something to complain about the same way she needed air to breathe. She might also have dipped into the dormant accounts to pay for the therapy.

Louise looked well. "You lost weight. Congratulations."

"Thanks. This diet works great."

"When's Stephanie coming home?"

"In a week."

And that's when the diet might stop working. Maybe not. Maybe I should phone my friend at the center and ask her to speak to the girl. Heart-to-heart talks didn't often work with teens, but maybe, just maybe, Stephanie would listen to the therapist.

At 5:15 I replaced the tapes. Mr. Bailey gave me the previous day's videos to look at. On the way home I treated myself to a pizza—vegetarian, to cut down on the calories, since I had skipped my pool workouts for several days. Tomorrow I'd swim no matter what.

I found no evidence of embezzling on the tapes. Had I nodded off during last night's viewing? Gritting my teeth, I looked at that tape again. Nothing.

Dumbfounded, I phoned Uncle Barney and told him what happened.

"You're sure that five thousand dollars was taken?"

"Positive. There's no mistake about that. But how? The embezzler has to use a computer to access the accounts, but none of the tellers' computers were used."

"Are there other terminals in the bank from which dormant accounts can be accessed?" Uncle Barney asked.

"Mr. Bailey's computer. Surely we can't suspect him."

"Not him. Just his terminal. How hard is it to get the access codes?"

"In most banks it would be nearly impossible, but at this branch security is relatively lax."

"We'll have to put a camera in his office. I'll call him and tell him."

"He'll hate it, but I'm sure he hates being ripped off even more. He's beginning to take this very personally."

"I'm beginning to take this personally," Uncle Barney said. "Foxy'll install the camera tonight."

After work I phoned Maxi. "How's the canvassing going?"

"My feet are killing me. I had to switch to my 'old-lady orthopedic' lace-ups."

"I'm sorry, Oma."

"Don't worry. I'm soaking my feet in a bucket of hot water and Epsom salt. Feels great." She sighed happily. "Anyway, I covered ten doctors' offices. None of them treated a dog bite wound. At least none would admit to it. But I can't imagine why they would lie to me."

"I can't either, especially since you're there with the dog who allegedly might have done the biting."

"I feel bad about that. I'm impugning Hiram's good name. But I explained to him why it was necessary."

"And he understood, did he?" I couldn't resist teasing.

Maxi laughed. "I know I'm being silly, talking to a dog."

"Better than talking to yourself. Not that you ever have," I added quickly.

"Want to come for supper?"

"I'd love to, but I have to talk to someone tonight." We spoke a little longer before I hung up.

The someone I had to talk to was Rafe. Where would I find him? He wasn't listed in the phone book. On Friday night I'd find him at the racetrack, but I didn't want to wait until then. Someone had mentioned that he hung out at The Last Drop, the bar down by the river. The way Sam had talked about it, the place wasn't one where I should go by myself.

Could I ask Luke? No. He'd be so protective that I wouldn't be able to talk to anybody. Glenn? He was on an out-of-town assignment. Then it hit me: Joan Bower. She'd gotten me on this case, so it was only fair that she should profit from some of the perks that came with it—like going to a shabby saloon.

She was surprisingly eager to go and promised to meet me in the bar's parking lot at nine.

Earlier that evening, we'd had one of those spectacular spring thunderstorms the Midwest was famous for. I skirted the water puddles in the parking lot.

"I hope I'm dressed okay," Joan said, holding her raincoat open for me to see her outfit.

She was wearing linen slacks and a short-sleeved, tailored blouse—a little conservative, perhaps, but a banker's idea of dressing down. "You look fine," I said.

I wore jeans and an unbuttoned, short-sleeved blouse over a red tank top.

"This is sort of exciting," she whispered as we approached the entrance.

"Yes, it is." Then I laughed. "We're pitiful, you know that? We're going into a third-rate bar and acting as if we were about to enter Rick's place in *Casablanca*."

"We need to get a life," Joan muttered.

"No kidding."

The first thing I noticed in The Last Drop was the smell. The pungent odor of stale beer almost made me gag. The second thing I noticed was the cigarette smoke that hung thick and heavy in the air.

"We should have brought some oxygen masks," Joan muttered.

"There's a table in the corner over there," I said and led the way, very conscious of the fact that everyone in the place was watching us.

"You'd think they've never seen a couple of women enter a bar before," Joan said as we sat down.

"I don't think it happens too often in here." We took our raincoats off and draped them over the back of the chairs.

The barmaid approached us. "What'll you ladies have?"

"A gin and—"

"We'll have two longnecks," I said quickly. After the woman left, I said, "In a place like this you don't want to order anything that's served in a glass."

Joan shuddered. "Good thinking." She looked around. "If this were a movie, there'd be at least one guy in here who looked a bit like the young cowboy in *Thelma and Louise.* Remember?"

"Brad Pitt. I remember. Well, that's the difference between movies and reality." I did a quick survey of the room.

"You see your young racer?"

"No, but it's early yet. He'll be in." I crossed my fingers under the table. I wasn't as sure as I sounded.

"I'm going to see what's on the jukebox." Joan dug some quarters out of her purse. "What would you like to hear?"

"Anything by Patsy Cline."

"Now there's a blast from the past."

"Her songs are classics. They'll have at least one on the jukebox."

When the first sweet, heartbreaking notes of "Crazy" floated from the jukebox, Rafe came in. Rather, he strutted in. Tonight he wore skintight jeans, ripped at the knees, boots, and a shirt halfway unbuttoned.

"Oh my," Joan said reverently. "Isn't he something."

"Yes, isn't he. And he's for sale."

"What do you mean?"

"He lost his sponsor. Car racing isn't cheap."

"How do you think the board of directors at the bank would react to my becoming his sponsor?"

I just flicked her a look.

"Yeah, that's what I thought too." She sighed.

After a moment's thought, I said, "On the other hand, do they need to know how you invest your own money?"

"No, they don't."

We watched Rafe flirt with the barmaid, watched a woman get up out of a booth, sidle up to him, and buy him a beer.

"What do you want to bet he doesn't have to buy a single beer tonight?" Joan asked.

"Or any night."

"Yeah."

When the barmaid returned to ask if we wanted another beer, we felt we had to say yes but also told her we wanted a word with Rafe.

"You and every other woman in the joint," she said sourly, but added that she'd relay the message.

A couple of minutes later, Rafe came to join us, carrying the two longnecks we'd ordered and his own.

"Ladies," he said, serving us. He turned a chair around, straddled it, and leaned his elbows on the back of it. He took a swig of beer.

"Thanks for bringing the beer," Joan said with a smile.

"Let me introduce you two," I said and did.

"Are you working in the bank too?" he asked Joan.

"Yes, I am."

"Well, I've never seen so many good-looking women in a bank before," Rafe said, smiling at Joan.

"Cybil tells me you race cars?" Joan asked.

"Yeah. On weekends. I'm getting a new car next week. You should come and see it."

"Maybe I will."

I let them talk and flirt a while, amusing myself by peeling the label off my first beer bottle, which I had barely touched. Eventually I interrupted them.

"Rafe, how long did you know Agnes?"

"Nine, no, ten months."

"How did you meet?"

"She came to the racetrack one afternoon when I was checking out my car. I can't remember who she came with." He grinned. "And one thing led to another."

"And you became more than friends, more than sponsor and racer?"

"Sure. Why not? We were both single, willing, and over twenty-one."

"But you weren't faithful to her, were you?"

"It wasn't that kind of arrangement. I'm not ready to settle down and Agnes knew that. I told her that up front."

"She was satisfied with that?"

"Sure. Why not?"

Joan and I exchanged a look. Men, especially young ones, could be so dense.

"When did you see her last?"

"Saturday night. She fixed dinner and then we went to a dance at the VFW. Agnes liked to dance."

"You didn't see her on Sunday?"

"No. I had a race downstate."

Where he met a woman and stayed over. His alibi.

Rafe rose and turned the chair around. "I would never have hurt Agnes. She was good to me. And I'm done answering questions."

We watched him walk back to the bar, as did every other woman in the place.

"I believe him," Joan said. "Don't you?"

"Yes, unfortunately."

"Why unfortunately?"

"Because I'm running out of suspects."

"When you catch the embezzler, you'll have a suspect."

"For the embezzling, but not necessarily for murder," I said and sighed. We left a few minutes later.

At nine o'clock the next morning I parked my car again in front of the convenience store. I figured by this time most people had gone to work and the stay-at-home moms had put their children on the school bus and were busy doing laundry or something.

Just in case, I had put on a pair of beige coveralls, a baseball cap, and carried a clipboard, which made me look sort of official, like a meter reader or municipal inspector of some sort. At least, that's the look I was going for.

I entered Agnes's house through the back door again. The first thing I did was close the window I had opened.

It had cooled off the house nicely. I did another walk-through to be sure no one else was in the house. I looked under the dining room table, my former hiding place, under the beds, and in the closets. Fortunately, the house didn't have a basement, so I was spared a walk down dark stairs.

The intruder had gone into one of the two bedrooms. Having no idea which one, I considered using the eenie-meeny-miny-moe rhyme to determine where I'd search first.

"Idiot," I muttered to myself and pushed the door to the front bedroom open. I had half expected the dresser drawers to be pulled out and their contents dumped on the floor, but the intruder had been remarkably neat in his search.

On first look everything looked untouched and orderly. The bed was neatly made, with a folded quilt lying across the foot. The Bible on the nightstand, the framed pictures on the dressing table, and the stack of photo albums on the chest of drawers looked the same. Yet something was different. Something small, something subtle.

I moved closer to inspect each piece of furniture. That's when I saw it. The slight layer of dust that had settled on the mahogany furniture allowed me to see that the photo albums had been moved a little to the left. The meager beam of the flashlight hadn't allowed the intruder to see the markings he'd left in the dust.

Also, it seemed to me that the stack of albums had been higher. Had the intruder taken one or two of them? There was only one person who could tell me if any of them were missing: Agnes's sister.

I dialed the bank on my cell phone. Mr. Bailey's secretary put me through to him.

"Mr. Bailey, do you know who Agnes's attorney is?"

"I don't think she had one. She appointed the bank to execute her will."

"I assume her sister is the beneficiary?"

"Cybil, I can't comment on that."

"Can you at least tell me when her sister is coming to town?"

"She'll be in the bank this afternoon."

"I need to ask her a question. Could I speak to her?"

"I have no objection."

"Thank you."

Briefly I looked at the other rooms but nothing struck me as being out of place or missing. I walked to my car and drove to the bank.

Not that I got much work done, feeling fidgety and vaguely apprehensive. It seemed to me I was no nearer to finding out who had killed Heather and Agnes than I had been days ago.

When Mr. Bailey finally called me to his office, it felt anticlimactic.

After Mr. Bailey explained that I was the one who had found her sister, Betty James agreed to meet me at

Agnes's house at 5:30. Betty didn't even ask why I wanted to meet her. Undoubtedly she was in shock at losing her sister in such a brutal fashion.

Since I arrived a few minutes early, I sat in the car until 5:30 on the dot. The family needed some time in the empty house to absorb the reality of Agnes's death. From experience I knew that knowing intellectually that a loved one had died was a long way from believing it on an emotional level.

Betty's husband and their two little girls went to sit in the backyard while I spoke with her.

"Could you please look at the albums in the front bedroom and tell me if any are missing?" I asked.

"That was my mother's bedroom, and the albums were hers." Betty seemed relieved that I hadn't asked her to go into Agnes's room.

"As you can see from the dust here, the albums were moved. That's why I'm wondering if any are missing," I explained.

"I'm surprised at the dust. Agnes was such a fussy housekeeper. I always thought she should have gotten married. She was a good cook and great around the house. Not that she didn't have any offers when she was young," Betty said quickly. "But she was choosy. Too choosy. And look where it got her." Betty suppressed a sob.

I didn't say anything and didn't look at her, giving her a chance to compose herself. If I had known her even slightly better, I'd have given her a hug.

She picked up the albums and looked at them. She frowned. "Why, yes. I believe there used to be more."

"Can you tell by looking at the photos which one is missing? I assume your mother arranged them in some kind of order?"

Betty nodded. "By years." She sat on the bed and looked at the first page of each album. When she was finished, she looked at me, puzzled.

"That's so weird. The two that are missing are from our high school years. Who'd be interested in them? Those are photos of us from over twenty years ago. I'd have thought if anybody was interested, they'd take the most recent albums."

"That is odd. Thank you, Betty. That's all I needed to know."

"Do you have any idea who . . . did this to Agnes?"

"No. At least not yet. But I will."

Brave, rash words, I reflected as I drove away. I had ruled out some people, but I had no idea who had done the crime. More and more I suspected that the motive for Agnes's murder was rooted in her past.

I returned to the bank to pick up the videotape from Mr. Bailey's office.

On my way home, I stopped at the Y and swam laps for thirty minutes. After I showered and changed into shorts and a T-shirt, I felt I was mentally and physically able to spend the evening watching a tape of bank transactions.

I fixed a simple meal of yogurt with fresh blueberries and whole wheat toast with peanut butter, which I ate while watching the tape. Since this was filmed after the bank had closed, I forwarded a huge chunk of tape. I was beginning to think that the embezzler had out-witted us somehow when movement on the tape made me sit up straight. I watched, practically open-mouthed. Then I stopped the tape and phoned Uncle Barney.

Ten minutes later he arrived at my house.

"Watch this," I said and pressed the PLAY button on the rewound tape.

A man entered Mr. Bailey's office, a ski mask pulled over his face. He rounded the desk quickly, sat down, turned the computer on, logged on—obviously know-ing the password—typed something in, and a few min-utes later logged off and left.

"I don't understand," Uncle Barney said. "He didn't get any cash."

"Yes, he did. Some time today, one of the tellers filled in a bogus withdrawal slip for the account he accessed and took the cash. I assume his co-embezzler gave it to him and received her cut."

Uncle Barney swore under his breath. "I'm getting tired of this."

Uncle Barney was an exceedingly patient man; if he was getting frustrated, no wonder I wanted to tear my hair out.

"Let's look at it again," he said, his tone grim.

We watched.

"Is there anything familiar about the guy?"

"With only the emergency lights on, it's very dim, but . . ." My voice trailed off.

"What, Cybil?"

"For a moment, as he turned, he reminded me of someone." I shook my head. "But who? Mr. Bailey is short and chubby, Edward limps, and the night watchman has a pronounced stoop. This man seems physically fit and strong." I paused, staring at the man whose image I had frozen by hitting the PAUSE button. He was only a dark outline. "Unless . . ."

"Unless what?"

"Unless it's one of the women tellers disguised as a man?"

"Run it again."

We both watched the figure's movements. I shook my head. "No. None of the women walk like that or are tall enough or big enough. If they'd put on padding, their movements would be a little stiff."

"You're right. We're dealing with a new element here. An outsider who knows about the bank. A boyfriend or a husband or a brother. Or just an accomplice." Barney reached for his pipe before he remembered that he didn't have it with him. "The question is, how did he get into the bank?"

"He must have the security code. Or he came in before closing and hid somewhere in the bank."

"Wouldn't he need the code to disarm the alarm when he left?"

"Yes. Unless he waited until we opened in the morning and then, pretending to be a customer, left. Or his teller accomplice smuggled him out." I paused, trying to think of alternatives, and couldn't. "What are we going to do now?"

"Stake out the place each night. One man on the inside, one out front, and one in the back."

"Which position do you want me to take?"

"I'll let you know."

Uncle Barney left, looking grim but determined.

I went to bed, my mind racing a mile a minute. Just before I fell asleep, something floated into my consciousness, but as I struggled to grasp its significance, it disappeared like a wisp of fog.

When the ringing of the telephone woke me, I felt as if I'd just fallen asleep. Glancing at the clock, I saw that I'd slept only an hour.

"Hello," I muttered. "Hello? Who's there?"

"It's me, Carol. You said I should call you if I ever needed help."

Carol? Carol from the bank. The abusive husband. "Are you hurt?"

"Yes, there's something wrong with my left arm."

"Where are you?"

"At the service station down the street from where I live."

"Give me the address." She did. "Stay there. Lock

yourself in the ladies' room, if necessary. Where's your husband?"

"At home. Probably passed out by now."

"I'll be there in ten minutes or less."

I didn't bother to put on a bra and was out of the house in two minutes.

Carol was waiting for me in the station's office, looking like a frightened little bird. She was holding her left arm against her body and her left eye was almost swollen shut. I put her in my car and took off for Westport General's emergency room.

Luke was on duty. When he heard I'd come in, he hurried out to meet us.

"Are you okay, Cybil?"

"Yes, but Carol here is not."

With gentle hands Luke examined her arm. "We're going to have to take some X-rays as soon as the nurse asks you a few questions."

Luke drew me aside. "How did her arm get broken? How did you get involved?"

"Carol works at the bank. And her drunken husband beat her again. That miserable louse!"

"Not all men are wife beaters," Luke said gently, "so don't give me those killer looks."

"Sorry. I just get so mad."

"I know."

"I told her to phone me when she was ready to do something about him."

"You're a good woman, Cybil Quindt." Luke smoothed back my hair.

Self-conscious about my mussed hair, I said, "I was asleep when she called. I didn't have time to comb it."

"It looks fine. We'll take it from here."

"You'll call the police?"

"You bet."

"Thanks, Luke."

Chapter Ten

W hile I was outside watering the flowers next morning, Maxi left a message on my answering machine. She had news and asked me to meet her at The Fragrant Grind for coffee.

I found her sitting at a sidewalk table, pouring water into a paper cup for Hiram.

"Hi, Hiram," I said to the dog, whose leash Maxi had clipped to the table leg. He wagged his tail.

Maxi waited until the waitress served the coffee before she spoke. "I wrote down everything as soon as I got to my car so I wouldn't forget anything." She took a small notebook, not unlike the one Sam used, from her purse.

"That reminds me. I have to talk to Sam," I said,

181

more to myself than to Maxi. "Go on. What did you find out?" I leaned forward expectantly.

"Well, Hiram and I were about to give up. We'd visited all the doctors' offices listed as family practices in the phone book except two. I mean, what are the chances of it being one of them?"

"Statistically very small," I agreed.

"One was on the west side of town and one on the south side. Both were located in what had at one time been private residences. Ranch-style houses."

I nodded encouragingly, though the architecture of the houses was immaterial.

"Since the south side one was on our way home, we stopped at the west side office first. They'd treated a snake bite, but no dog bites."

"So it was the last office on your list?"

"Naturally. Murphy's Law or something like that."

Maxi paused to sip coffee. Judging by her facial reaction, the coffee was good. She was very picky about coffee.

"Anyway, the receptionist remembered me from the library. Years ago she used to bring her kids to story hour. Funny how many people I run into who remember me from the library."

"Because you were friendly and helpful to your clients. An exemplary librarian."

"Nice of you to say so, *Schatzi*. Where was I? Oh yes. The receptionist recalled the guy because he paid in cash, and the nurse remembered him because he was such a baby. Wouldn't let her give him a tetanus shot."

"Really?"

"Even after she explained to him why he should have one. Since he refused, they cleaned the wound and rebandaged it."

"I guess you can't force somebody to get a shot," I said.

"I wouldn't worry too much. It wasn't much of a bite. The guy wore jeans and you know how tough denim is. And he wore thick socks. And Hiram is a small dog."

"Small but brave," I added for his benefit.

"Isn't he, though?" Maxi petted him. "Oh, you should know that I called the vets in the area and located the one who treated Hiram. My little sweetie is up on his shots."

"That's good news. You have been busy."

Maxi smiled, pleased.

"What name did the man give the doctor?"

"Ian Smythe."

I groaned. "That's a variation of John Smith. Doesn't anybody have any imagination?"

"Apparently not. Too much television watching and not enough reading."

"What did this Ian look like?"

Maxi consulted her notebook. "I quote: 'Sort of average. Average height and weight.' Upper middle age. Brown hair and mustache. Glasses with thin gold rims."

"That's it?"

"Yes."

"Not much to go on. This description probably fits a lot of guys. And the mustache and glasses could be a disguise." I sighed. "It's probably too much to hope for that anyone saw what kind of car he drove?"

"I asked that question. The receptionist glanced out when he left because he'd refused the shot and she was upset. She thinks he drove off in a dark blue SUV."

There was that dark-colored SUV again. Unfortunately, they weren't exactly a rarity.

"Does any of this help?" Maxi asked.

"It will later when we're tying up loose ends. Thanks, Oma. You and Hiram did a good job."

My grandmother beamed with pleasure.

While I sipped coffee, I came to a decision. "I'll have to go to the racetrack. Maybe I can get something out of him."

"Who's the 'him' and what do you need from him?"

"The him is Rafe. Agnes's boyfriend. He's getting his rebuilt racecar today."

"And you suspect him of . . . what?"

"I'm not sure. Not of murder, but he is the reason Agnes embezzled money."

"She paid for this rebuilt car?"

"Yes."

"I'll go with you. That is, I'll follow you in my car. It's not out of the way. Or just a little bit."

Maxi wore that determined look that told me nothing

I said could dissuade her. Besides, how dangerous could it be in broad daylight? And I liked spending time with her.

While driving there I was careful not to let any cars pull in between us, though chances of my grandmother getting lost were slim. She'd lived in Westport since she'd immigrated to the United States from Austria in 1938.

We parked in the grassy area. I was amazed how many people were at the track. Not only the cleanup company tidying up after last night's race, but mechanics and drivers working on cars and plenty of guys just standing around and watching. What was it with men and machines?

With Hiram on his leash, we walked around the track until we found Rafe, surrounded by a bunch of men, all admiring his new car. It looked small, even fragile, to my untrained eyes and I caught myself thinking that no amount of money could persuade me to drive that flimsy thing around the oval as fast as it could go.

"It doesn't look very substantial," Maxi whispered, echoing my thoughts.

"I guess maybe it's supposed to be light so it can go fast?" I shrugged. Neither one of us knew much about cars. And I didn't really want to know about them. As long as they started and drove smoothly, I was happy.

Eventually Rafe caught sight of me. He did a double take and then walked over to join us. I introduced Maxi.

"What do you ladies think?" he asked, pointing proudly at the car.

"It looks like it could get the job done," Maxi said diplomatically.

"Oh, yes. Agnes would have been so proud. She had great hopes for it. She was the one who insisted we buy it."

"Pardon me for asking, but how could you afford it?"

"Agnes said she'd get the money from the bank. A loan, I guess. She was the financial genius. She took care of the money."

She certainly did.

Somebody called his name. "Excuse me, ladies. I gotta go. If you come next Friday, you'll see this baby in action."

Without a word, we walked toward our parked cars.

"Could she have taken out a bank loan?" Maxi asked.

"She didn't at her bank. And I'm fairly sure she didn't anywhere else. I found no loan papers among her stuff. Bankers are conservative and car racing is risky."

Maxi nodded. "So she took the money from the bank without going through the proper procedures. Didn't she think she'd get caught?"

"Apparently not. Sam says all criminals think they're smart and won't get caught."

"Or she didn't care. Thought he was worth it," Maxi said.

"Agnes must have been a risk-taker."

Maxi shook her head. "I've never understood that mentality."

I didn't either. I suspected I was basically a chicken rather than a hawk.

We parted in the parking lot, Maxi to drive to her farm and I to my house.

Sam was on duty on Sunday, so after church I drove to the police station. I had baked raisin-oatmeal cookies to take to Sunday school, and, knowing how much Sam liked them, I put a half dozen into a brown bag that I set on his desk.

He didn't say anything until after he had looked inside the bag. "You know that bribing a police officer is a crime?"

"Who's bribing an officer?" I said, making a production of looking around the office. "I merely brought my cousin a few cookies. Don't tell me the state of Indiana has made that a crime."

"Why didn't you say you were here in a cousinly capacity?" Sam bit into a cookie and nodded his approval.

I sat in his visitor's chair and waited until he'd eaten a couple of cookies. He brushed cookie crumbs from his tie.

"And you're here because? Let me guess: to ask about the Agnes Miller case."

"Is there anything new? Anything you want to share?"

"Anything *you* want to share? You worked with the woman."

"You've talked with her boyfriend?"

"Yes. His alibi checks out."

I nodded. "It wouldn't make sense for him to hurt Agnes. She was good to him."

Sam raised a blond eyebrow. "People kill people who're good to them. That's no guarantee. But as I said, he's got a firm alibi."

"Any leads at all?" I asked.

Sam nodded. "A partial print in the bedroom. Don't ask," he said, holding up his hand. "I can't say any more."

"Actually, I came to ask about something else. Remember I mentioned the woman I work with whose fifteen-year-old daughter was dating a man twice her age?"

Sam snapped his fingers. "I've been meaning to call you about him."

I watched him flip through several stacks of papers on his desk. It took all my self-control not to suggest that he use some sort of filing system. On second thought, he always found what he looked for, so maybe he used a system that made sense to him but was a mystery to the rest of us.

"Here's the note. One Deacon Harris. Got in a bar fight, resisted arrest, and slugged a cop. He's going to be a guest of the state for quite a while. Your friend's daughter will be safe from him."

"Thank heaven. And thank you, Sam." I felt incredibly relieved to be able to give Louise this good news. I rose. Then I remembered. "One more thing. There was a car accident a block from Agnes's house a couple of nights ago. It involved an SUV. How can I find out to whom it belongs?"

"You can't. I can. Why do you want to know?"

"That SUV keeps turning up."

Sam frowned. "I don't like the sound of that. I'll check it out."

"Thank you."

Since the bank was the executor of Agnes's estate, Sam had given me permission to go into her house. Agnes's sister had made funeral arrangements but since the police wouldn't release the body yet, she and her family had gone back to Chicago.

I entered the house by the back door. The stale air hit me as soon as I entered. The house was beginning to have that abandoned, closed-up smell.

As I walked down the hall, the telephone rang. I stopped to listen to the machine pick up the message. I don't know what I expected, but felt disappointed when the message was from the photo department of the drugstore, reminding Agnes that her pictures were ready. I made a mental note to pick them up and give them to her sister.

While I placed the photo albums on the dining room table to look at them, it seemed to me that the stack was bigger. Had the missing albums been returned? My scalp prickled. I looked around. When had the intruder returned the albums? Was he still in the house?

I picked up the albums and made myself walk normally to the back door. As soon as I was outside, I sprinted to my car. Without a wasted motion I dumped them into the back seat, started the engine, and took off, burning rubber like a teenager.

What was in the albums that was important enough to risk breaking and entering, not once but twice? Except the intruder hadn't broken in. He apparently had a key. Had he stolen it? Had Agnes given it to him? In either case, he had known Agnes.

Who was he? Both Sam and I had ruled out Rafe. From what I knew about Agnes, and I felt that by now I knew a lot, her life didn't include many men other than relatives and those who worked at the bank. That included Mr. Bailey, Edward, and the night watchman. The night watchman? Now I was really grasping at straws. The man was seventy-five if he was a day and a retired bank custodian. Edward limped, and Mr. Bailey was the boss.

Other than her brother-in-law, who obviously didn't know Agnes well and admittedly saw her once or twice a year at festive gatherings, the family included only a couple of elderly uncles who lived in Michigan. All the way up on the Upper Peninsula. I was back to square one. I had worked on cases where there was an abundance of suspects but never on one where there were none. Or rather, none that I could see. What was I missing?

I placed the albums on my kitchen table and made myself look through them. I paid special attention to the two that had been missing. The glue on some of the photos had dried and they had come loose from the backing. Or had they? Maybe the intruder had pried them loose. Maybe he thought something had been written on the back? Or been hidden behind them? I found nothing.

The snapshots themselves were normal, candid shots, sometimes out of focus, sometimes poorly framed—in short, everyday family pictures. The only thing they had in common was the time frame: Agnes's teenage years. And the location: her hometown on the U.P.

Pushing the albums away from me, I leaned my elbows on the kitchen table and cradled my head in the palms of my hands. I allowed myself a few minutes of self-pity.

Okay. So I was temporarily stuck and didn't know what to do next. There was always housework. I put on my painter's cap and proceeded with the kitchen cabinets. The shade of basil green had been a great choice.

Since no one had told me differently, I reported for work at the bank. On the way I stopped at the drugstore and picked up Agnes's photos. I stuck the yellow envelope into my purse.

Mr. Bailey looked like he hadn't slept well in days. The continued embezzling was getting to him.

"Any news?" he asked, obviously hoping for a favorable report.

I shook my head. "But it's only a matter of time. Was there anything familiar about the man in the video?"

"No." He paused, frowning. "And yet. . . ." His voice trailed off. "I can't put my finger on it but there was a moment when I thought there was something familiar about him."

I nodded. "I know what you mean. I had the same reaction. But why?"

We looked at each other, both feeling totally frustrated.

"If it's okay with you, I'll keep monitoring the dormant accounts until we catch the embezzler," I said.

"Do that. I hope to high heaven that's soon."

So did I.

By five o'clock I had interviewed three candidates for Agnes's position. Mr. Bailey hired one of them. I cleared my desk and waited for 5:30, when I would replace the videotapes and check the dormant accounts.

While I waited, I opened the envelope containing Agnes's photos, expecting snapshots of Rafe at the racetrack. Instead I found three copies of one small snapshot. At first I glanced disinterestedly at the picture of a man in a bathing suit standing on a beach. Then it hit me: I knew this man, but there was something very wrong with the photo.

My mouth felt dry, my throat was tight, my heart hammered. With shaking hands I reached for the phone and dialed the ER number. The nurse put me through to Luke.

"I need the answers to a couple of questions."

"Cybil. I'm fine. Thanks for asking."

"I'm sorry, Luke. I didn't mean to be abrupt but this is important."

"You sound almost frantic. Where are you?"

"I am still at the bank and I am almost frantic. I've discovered something."

"Go ahead and ask your question," Luke said, his tone sober.

I had to take a calming breath before I could speak. "Okay. If someone says they've had polio as a child, and they limp, wouldn't the affected leg look different than the healthy one?"

"Yes, it would. The muscle bulk would be severely reduced. The leg would look thinner, weaker. The word usually used to describe such a leg is *wasted*. Why are you asking?"

"Because I'm looking at a photo of a man standing on what I think is a beach on Lake Michigan and both of his legs look strong and healthy, even though he claims he had polio as a child and even though he usually affects a limp."

"You said the operative word: *affects*. I don't know why he's lying about having had polio as a child but he is."

A slight noise at the door made me look up. The door swung open. Edward stood there. My heart skipped a beat. How much had he heard? He motioned for me to hang up.

I turned half away. "The affected is here," I murmured, hoping Luke would hear and understand. I hung up.

"You're working late too," I said, pretending everything was just fine.

"What's going on? You're working late again," he said with a frown. "No trainee has ever worked that many hours."

"I don't mind," I said, trying to sound breezy.

"If you remember, I'm the supervisor and I say who gets overtime."

"Oh, I'm not on the clock. I'm staying late on my own time, trying to get everything done."

"What do you need to get done?"

He had me there. Why hadn't I prepared a plausible story? I pretended to have a coughing fit to gain time. "Pardon me," I said, reaching for a tissue. "Mr. Bradley asked me to check these accounts." I waved my hand at the stack of computer printouts, hoping they actually contained columns of figures. This being a bank, chances were good that this was the case.

Being the control freak that he was, Edward picked up the printouts. He frowned at them. "Why would Mr. Bailey ask you to look at these? They are three months old."

I shrugged and tried for the slightly surprised who-knows-what-bosses-think look. Then I realized that the photos were on the desk. Without breaking eye contact, I moved my left arm over them, hoping that the sleeve of my blouse hid them.

"I don't like people wandering around the bank after hours," Edward said.

"Oh, I wasn't wandering around, just sitting at my desk."

"Time to go," he commanded.

If I got up, he wouldn't fail to see the photos. "Fine. Let me just straighten my desk and then I'll leave."

"It looks tidy to me. Come. I'll walk you out."

He was bound and determined to stand there and watch me. Using my right hand, I eased my desk drawer open as far as I could, still sitting down. Slowly I moved my left arm toward me, hoping to slide the pictures into the drawer. It worked with two of them, but the third one stuck to the blotter.

"What do you have there?"

"Nothing. Just some photos," I said and swept them into the drawer.

"Let me see them."

"They're private. They wouldn't interest you," I said but he must have caught a glimpse of them. Before I could close the drawer, he was beside me. His hand shot out to keep the drawer from closing. "Really. They're just some snapshots," I repeated desperately.

I never noticed what large, strong hands Edward had

until then. Unbidden, the image of those hands closing around Agnes's throat rose before my eyes, making me shiver.

He took the photos and glanced at them. I tried to get up, but he placed his left hand on my shoulder, holding me down.

"So, that bitch Agnes got hold of the photos and blackmailed me. Bad luck for her. And bad luck for you. How'd you get them anyway?"

"A call from the drugstore photo department. I thought they'd be family snapshots and Agnes's sister might want them, so I picked them up."

He made a clucking sound. "Too bad. I liked you. But I have no choice now."

"I don't understand what the big deal is. Who cares that you had polio?"

"The draft board, that's who."

I tried to recall the last time the draft board had been active. "Vietnam? Your number was coming up?"

"Yeah."

"I still don't understand. How could you fool the draft board?"

"My cousin had polio. I mailed his medical records and letters from the doctors. It wasn't that I was a coward. I wasn't. I wasn't afraid to die, but I just couldn't stand the idea of slogging through the jungle, of being hot and dirty and smelly." He shuddered delicately.

"So you fooled the draft board. And then you had to go on with the masquerade of pretending to be crippled. Wasn't that worse than the chance of getting drafted? And how did you pull it off?"

"I moved away from home. Never went back. Never got in touch with anybody back home. And people don't ask questions about a handicap."

"How did Agnes find out?"

"She didn't. Heather did. I made the mistake of once taking off my brace and going out on the beach. It was miles from here. Just my bad luck that Heather was out on a boat with her boyfriend. She saw me and took photos."

"Did she blackmail you?"

"No. Heather just toyed with me, holding the threat of exposure over me. Made her feel powerful."

"So you put the sleeping pills in her drink." Heather would have let him into her apartment, not suspecting that the seemingly harmless head teller and her erstwhile mentor could turn killer on her.

"I thought that would be the end of it, but apparently Heather had shown the photos to Agnes, and Agnes needed money, so she blackmailed me. Bled me dry."

"Why didn't you just use the dormant accounts to pay her off?"

"She was already using them. She was never going to stop blackmailing me. That boyfriend of hers would always need money. There'd be no end to the demands. I got sick to death of being exploited."

"Where did you get the ether you used on me?"

"From my cousin, the pharmacist."

Edward turned slightly and hitched his shoulder. That was the movement in the video that had struck both Mr. Bailey and me as familiar. What now?

"Get up," he ordered.

"No. I think I'll stay right here and wait for my husband."

Before I could do anything, he jerked me into a standing position as if I were a limp bundle of rags.

"You'll do as I say or really, really regret it."

His eyes bored into mine. How come I had never noticed how totally malicious his little pig eyes were? They raised goosebumps on my arms.

He stuffed the photos into his pocket. "You're coming with me."

"I don't think so." Next thing I knew he had taken a snub-nosed gun from his pocket and pointed it at me.

When he pulled my hair hard, the pain forced me to stand up and walk with him. Tears of pain pooled in my eyes but I wouldn't give him the satisfaction of seeing me cry.

"We're going to walk out of here like we were the best of friends."

I wanted to tell him where to go but knew that my words would only earn me new pain. For now I'd do as I was told. At some point there would be a moment when I could get away from him. I'd have to or die. I was sure of that. The only question was where, how, and when.

"We're going for a ride." He released my hair, but,

pressing the gun against my ribs, he marched me through the deserted bank to the parking lot. The whole time I prayed for the guard to show up.

As if he could read my mind, Edward said, "If we meet the guard, act natural or I'll shoot him. I mean it."

I believed him. He had already killed Heather and Agnes. One or two more bodies didn't matter. The state of Indiana could execute him only once.

Luckily, we met no one. He made me get into the car on the passenger side. By the time I'd crawled over the gear box, he was seated, the gun pointing steadily at me.

"Where's the SUV you've been driving?" I asked.

"At home in the garage. Now drive. Nice and slow. You attract the attention of a cop, I'll shoot him first and then you."

I swallowed. "Where are we going?"

"I'll give you directions as we go."

He did. Before long, I knew we were headed for the same lake he'd tried to drown me in once before. My heartbeat accelerated and my palms were damp as they gripped the steering wheel. *Breathe slow and deep*, I told myself. He didn't succeed the first time and he wouldn't now. Except he had a gun. True, it was a small one, probably a .22-caliber. Still, at close range it could kill me.

I needed to make my move soon. We were approaching Washington Street, which was lined with big round concrete flower planters. If I could sideswipe one of those. . . . For that I needed to get into the right lane. I did, ignoring the horn blasts that followed my move.

"What in the world?" he exclaimed. "Don't do that again."

"You shoot me while I'm at the wheel, you'll get hurt too. Maybe even killed. Think about that," I said, my bravado surprising even me.

"Stupid bitch. Drive carefully."

The traffic light turned red and I stopped the car.

Could I jump out and get away before he could shoot me?

"Don't even think of bolting," he warned. "You'll never make it."

Okay, then. Edward had made the decision for me. When the light turned green, I accelerated slowly to allow the car in front of me to get a head start. Then, taking a deep breath, I stomped on the gas pedal. The moment I reached thirty miles an hour I swerved and aimed the right side of the car at the next concrete planter. We hit hard enough to create a satisfying crunching of metal. The hood popped up and steam escaped from the radiator.

I had braced myself, knowing what I was going to do. Edward hadn't and was thrown hard against the dashboard. I jumped out of the car. Dodging traffic, I ran across the street and sprinted in the direction of my uncle's agency.

After two blocks my lungs threatened to burst and the sharp stitch in my side was excruciatingly painful. I should have taken up jogging instead of swimming.

Glancing back, I was shocked to see Edward in hot pursuit.

I heard a popping noise. The display window of the dress shop I was passing splintered. It took a second before I realized what was happening: Edward was shooting at me. Lucky for me, he didn't seem to be a crack shot.

Didn't anybody see what was going on? I saw two women jump behind a parked car. I thought I heard screams but by now my breathing was so loud it dimmed all other sounds.

I had almost reached the agency when I saw the window beside its entrance shatter. Lynn would have a fit. She would probably charge me to get it fixed. The door suddenly opened. I tried to warn Uncle Barney but all I uttered were incoherent sounds. It didn't matter; he saw what was going on. As he ducked down, his arm pulled me inside, where I collapsed on the floor.

When I looked up, I saw him aim his revolver and shoot.

Then he knelt beside me and put his arms around me.

"It's okay. That man won't hurt you. He'll never hurt anyone again."